PRAISE FOR STEPHEN LEATHER

'A writer at the top of his game'
Sunday Express

'A master of the thriller genre'
Irish Times

'Let Spider draw you into his
web, you won't regret it'
The Sun

'The sheer impetus of his storytell-
ing is damned hard to resist'
Daily Express

'High-adrenaline plotting'
Sunday Express

'Written with panache, and a fine ear for dia-
logue, Leather manages the collision between
the real and the occult with exceptional skill,
adding a superb time-shift twist at the end'
Daily Mail on *Nightmare*

ROGUE WARRIOR

Rogue Warrior

Stephen Leather

CHAPTER 1

A sagging chainlink fence was strung between the sheer rock faces at the quarry entrance and the steel gates were held shut by a thick, rusty chain and padlock. The weathered sign 'GRAINGER QUARRY' dangling from the fence rattled in the fitful gusts of wind stirring dust devils from the quarry floor. An overhead conveyor belt led from the rock face to a giant hopper near the gates. In its shadow was a truck already loaded with hardcore for the next day's first delivery run. It was parked next to the site office, a rough shack built of scrap timber and corrugated steel. The magazine at the foot of the quarry wall was a much more solid construction, made of armoured steel and fitted with a high security padlock.

An owl perched on the edge of the conveyor, the wind ruffling its feathers as it scanned the quarry floor for the scuttling movements of its prey. Suddenly it swivelled its head towards the deep pool of darkness where the fence met the overhanging rock wall. It took flight on soundless wings as a figure detached himself from the shadows and began crossing the open ground towards the magazine. A ski mask obscured his features and he was clad from head to foot in black. His movements were slow and silent, each measured footfall barely disturbing the dust.

His friends, and acquaintances, called him Shorty - very few people knew his real name. He'd had a career, a home, friends and a family once, but all those ties had long since been broken. In the past two years he had barely spoken to a soul, while the anger inside him burned ever hotter.

When Shorty reached the magazine he paused and took a long look around him, listening intently. There was the dull glint of moonlight on blue metal as he pulled a bunch of flat picks from his pocket. They were made from the metal from mini hacksaw blades, filed as thin as kitchen skewers but with the strength and pliability to move the internal workings of a heavy-duty industrial lock. He had made them many years before as part of another life, clamping the blades in a vice and breaking off the lugs from either end that fitted into the frame of a hacksaw. He then filed off all but two of the saw teeth and reshaped the remaining ones to fit the levers of locks. He bent a couple of right angles into the other end of the blades, giving his picks more spring and making it easier to maintain tension on a lock. He stooped over the lock, using a pick held in his left hand to keep tension on the locking bar while he forced up the levers of the padlock with the others.

As he worked, he kept his eyes closed, allowing nothing to disturb his focus on the feel of the thin steel picks in his hand. He was close to springing the lock when he felt the cold muzzle of a pistol pressed into his back. 'Get your hands up, punk. You're under arrest.'

The voice sounded young and there was a tremor of nerves and excitement in it. Shorty straightened up, still feeling the pressure of the pistol against his spine. His mind was clear and cold, his pulse steady and even. An older, more experienced guard would have kept two or three paces back as he challenged the intruder. With the confidence of youth, this guard thought that because he held a pistol, he was in control. He had already made the mistake that would cost him his life.

Shorty leaned back a fraction against the muzzle of the guard's pistol, pushing it down into the small of his back, and raised his hands in apparent surrender. As he did so, he glanced over his shoulder, to make sure the guard was not faking it with two fingers against the spine while he held the pistol back in his other hand.

The glance told Shorty all he needed to know. He continued to raise his hands and pivoted on the ball of his left foot, dropping his left arm as he swung round to sweep the gun out and away. In the same movement he swung his right fist, smashing it straight into the guard's throat. The only noise was the thud of the blow. With his larynx destroyed and his windpipe blocked, the guard could neither shout nor breathe.

He was already helpless but Shorty still carried on the fluid movement. As the guard began to fall backwards, his assailant's right hand followed through from the punch to seize his hair and jerk him forward again until he was almost bent double. The left hand swung down to strike at the top of the guard's spine. The impact of the blow with Shorty's extended second knuckle dislodged one of the discs and severed the spinal chord. The guard was dead within seconds.

Still holding onto the hair, Shorty lowered the body soundlessly to the ground. As the body gave a last convulsive jerk and lay still, Shorty released his grip on the hair and slid his hand down to the neck, using his forefinger in a final check for a pulse at the carotid artery. There was none. In the space of a single heartbeat the guard had gone from standing with a gun at the intruder's back to lying dead as stone at his feet. The only noises had been the impacts of the two blows, barely audible above the sound of the wind. Shorty was not even breathing hard.

He looked around, raking the shadows with his gaze. Nothing moved. He was annoyed with himself, because he had allowed the guard to surprise him and knew he had been lucky to escape so easily, but he had no regrets for the guard's fate; he was just one more obstacle to be overcome. He crouched down again and searched the dead man's pockets. There was a bunch of keys including one that he guessed would unlock the padlock on the main gates, but there was no key for the lock on the magazine; site security was slack, but not that slack.

He stepped over the body and resumed work on the padlock. After a few more minutes' work there was a faint click and it dropped open. He swung the door of the magazine wide, stepped inside and shone the shielded, narrow beam of his torch around the shelves. The magazine was almost empty. It contained only two blasting caps and two four-ounce sticks of plastic explosive, but it would be enough for his purposes.

He shoved the sticks of plastic explosive into his pockets, showing no more concern than if they had been two bits of wood, but he treated the blasting caps with considerable caution. PE was nothing to worry about - in the past, he had even boiled water by burning pieces of it - but blasting caps were an altogether different proposition. A spark or even a little too much heat could easily detonate them. They were the size of a pen top with two, foot-long trailing electric wires. He made sure that the exposed ends of the wires to each cap were twisted tightly around each other, then placed them in a tin lined with foam rubber. He slipped it into his breast pocket.

He left the door of the magazine open and put the padlock in his pocket, then dragged the body over to the gates. He opened them with the key from the guard's pocket and dumped the body outside, then swept away his tracks with a branch from a fir tree. He took off his sneakers and squeezed his feet into the dead man's smaller size boots, then walked across the quarry to the magazine and back to the gates.

Still moving at the same measured, unhurried pace, he changed back into his own shoes and walked off down the hill. The Jeep Cherokee he had stolen from a commuter station parking lot earlier that day was hidden in the undergrowth at the side of the dirt road a quarter of a mile away. Driving without lights, he went back up the hill to the quarry gates, dumped the body into the back of the Jeep, and then drove away into the night, watched only by the owl returning to its vantage point high above the deserted quarry.

The following night a ready-mix concrete truck was stolen from a construction company in New Jersey. The thief drove it to a farm on the outskirts of a hick town in Pennsylvania. He parked by the side of the track leading to the farm buildings and walked off into the darkness. After a couple of minutes a dog barked and a light was switched on in an upper window of the farmhouse. There was no visible movement and no other sound than the barking dog. It was abruptly silenced. A few moments later, the kitchen light went on in the house and an old farmer clutching a shotgun, opened the door and peered out into the darkness. 'Who's there?' he said. 'Show yourself or I'll shoot.'

There was the Phttt! Phttt! sound of two muffled shots fired in rapid succession from a silenced gun and the farmer slumped to the ground. All was then silent.

When Shorty re-emerged from the darkness, he clambered up into the cab of the truck and backed it up to a huge hopper in the yard. He loaded several tons of fertiliser into the drum of the truck, then drove round to the tank where the farmer stored the diesel for his tractors and machinery, and pumped scores of gallons on top of the fertiliser. As he drove off into the darkness, the great drum of the truck slowly revolved, glinting in the moonlight.

CHAPTER 2

It was a burning hot late summer's morning and there were sweat stains on the shirt of the guard manning the barrier at the entrance to the Convention Centre's underground parking lot. The tinny sound of his battered radio competed with the idling diesel engine of a beer delivery truck waiting at the barrier. 'This is 700WLW Newstalk, Ohio's top news station. The NRA Annual Meeting gets under way this morning at the downtown convention centre.' The presenter's tone of voice and stilted delivery showed he was reading from a PR hand-out. 'This national event includes fifteen acres of the most spectacular display of firearms, shooting and hunting accessories in the world, and is expected to bring thousands of out of state visitors to town, giving a multi-million dollar boost to the local economy. It's the greatest gun show on earth, folks, so come along yourselves, bring the whole family along and join in with what our friends at the NRA promise will be a weekend of fellowship and fun. We'll be talking to the NRA President a little later this morning, but the latest word on the traffic from Wanda, our eye in the sky, is up next, right after these messages.'

Just as the ad-break began, the guard leaped to his feet as he saw a ready-mixed concrete truck roaring down the entry ramp. The delivery truck was still blocking the entrance and a pick-up truck had just pulled up at the exit barrier and was waiting for it to lift when the concrete truck appeared. The guard caught a momentary glimpse of its driver, a man in a hooded sweatshirt and a grubby baseball cap, before it smashed into the back of the beer truck. Fully laden with barrels of beer for the convention, it was a formidable obstacle and although the impact pushed it a few yards further down the ramp, as the squeal of tortured metal drowned all other noise, the concrete truck came to a juddering halt, jammed between the beer truck and the concrete bollards surrounding the guard-post.

The delivery truck driver's neck was whiplashed by the impact and he slumped across the wheel of his truck, but the driver of the concrete truck was unhurt. He jumped out of his cab and ran back up the ramp. Although almost paralysed with shock, the guard was also uninjured and within seconds he had hit the alarm and the panic button connecting the convention centre to the Police Department.

The engine of the concrete truck was still running and the guard climbed up into the cab and switched off the ignition. In that instant the whole truck exploded, killing him instantly. The blast obliterated the beer truck and severely damaged the cars parked near the foot of the ramp, but because it had taken place partly in the open on the entrance ramp, much of the force of the explosion and its shock wave was dissipated. Had it detonated deep within the parking lot, next to the elevator shafts it might have collapsed the entire building. As it was, it spread most of its destruction over the area just outside the convention centre.

As if emphasising the random, almost capricious impact of the explosion, some passers-by were unscathed while their companions were injured or killed. A seven-year-old boy had been walking along the sidewalk hand in hand with his parents. They had arrived from Arecibo in Puerto Rico three weeks before. Both parents were killed instantly, but the boy, although orphaned in a split second, was not even scratched. Two visiting British businessmen were also killed when a lump of falling debris crushed the back of the taxi in which they were travelling past the convention centre. The driver was injured but would have survived, had the shock not brought on a fatal heart attack.

A Toyota saloon ran into the wreckage of the taxi. The passenger side airbag failed to inflate and the passenger, a 19-year old young woman from Des Moines, Iowa, in town for the regional finals of the Miss America pageant, who was not wearing her seat belt, was propelled through the windshield. She survived but her left arm was later amputated and her face scarred for life.

The death toll eventually reached eleven, but remarkably, although some of the NRA delegates in the arms fair and auditorium on the upper floors of the convention centre were among the 42 injured, none were killed. Prayers of thanks were given for their deliverance, which born again NRA members were already hailing as evidence of Divine Intervention to protect the righteous.

CHAPTER 3

Shorty was wearing a chauffeur's uniform and holding an expensive-looking lunchbox as he approached the main doors of the Virginia Academy. Not far from the banks of the Potomac separating Virginia from Washington DC, it was a very exclusive school, where class size was guaranteed not to exceed a dozen pupils, of whom 95 per cent were white and 100 per cent were rich. A guard just inside the entrance doors presided over a metal detector through which, even in this exclusive bastion of WASP privilege, all students and visitors had to pass.

Shorty half-walked and half-ran up the steps to the entrance. As the guard eyed him suspiciously, he held up the executive lunch box. 'Master James has forgotten his lunch. He has gluten intolerance and other problems, so cook always prepares his meals special for him,' Shorty said, the words tumbling out of him in his apparent haste. 'Could I just get this to him?'

The guard shrugged. 'Sorry, no can do. If you're not a student or a parent I recognise, I can't let you in here without authorisation.'

'Man, help me out here,' Shorty said. 'You don't know what my boss is like. I'll be fired if I don't get it to the boy. At least let me leave it at the office for him. It's just along the corridor there, right? Come on,' he said, as he saw the guard hesitate. 'I'll never be out of your sight all the way there and back.'

The guard thought about it a moment longer, and then said 'All right, but make it snappy, you hear?'

'Thanks man, you're a real life-saver.' As he walked past the guard, the scanner began to sound.

'Sorry,' Shorty said, as the guard's hand went to the butt of his pistol. 'I forgot about this.' He pulled a gunmetal cigarette case from his back pocket. 'It was my daddy's, he took it to war with him in Vietnam, and I did the same in I-raq. It's only got smokes in it.' He handed it to the guard, who fumbled with the catch to open it.

As he did so, Shorty whipped a combat knife from the sheath at the back of his belt, clamped his hand over the guard's mouth and drove the knife up under his rib-cage and into his heart. He held the guard until his eyes rolled up into his head, then lowered him to the ground. Shorty's pulse had barely risen from its resting rate. He retrieved the cigarette case, took the guard's weapon, checked the magazine and picked up an extra clip from the shelf in the guard's cubicle, then walked down the hallway.

The school secretary glanced up as he reached the open doorway of the office. 'Can I help you?'

His swift glance covered the room, taking in the secretary, her assistant and the closed door leading to the principal's office. He stepped through the doorway, shot both women in the head at no more than two yards range, splattering blood and brains all over the wall, then, with the same unhurried gait, strode to the principal's office, opened the door and shot him as he was still rising from his seat. He went back into the corridor, ignored the first classroom door he passed, then entered the next. The teacher turned to face him, a question on his lips that would now forever be unanswered. Shorty shot him and every single one of the dozen children in the room, while they tried to scramble for cover beneath their desks, screaming their terror. He even took time to change magazines before killing the rest of them.

He turned and walked back down the corridor, pausing at the office long enough to remove the hard disk drive containing the CCTV images. He slipped it into his pocket, then switched off the CCTV cameras, dropped the guard's gun to the floor and walked out of the school as pandemonium erupted behind him.

The killings, including the daughter of a prominent Republican senator, dominated the news that night, with politicians queuing up to comment. As always in the wake of a high school massacre, Democrats called for tighter gun controls, while the Republicans urged more armed guards to protect schools. NRA spokesmen kept their heads down for a couple of days and then, as the media circus started to move on to the next hot topic, they began their familiar litany: 'Guns don't kill people; people kill people. We don't need fewer guns in school, we need more of them and better training for those carrying them'.

CHAPTER 4

As the bell rang for recess and her class stampeded for the door, Grace Howard wiped the whiteboard clean, gathered up her papers and walked down the corridor to the staffroom. While her colleagues helped themselves to coffee and separated into their usual groups, talking about last night's TV or their problems with troublesome pupils and their equally troublesome parents, Grace took a soda, sat in the corner and opened her book. She was in her forties, with brown hair tinged with grey and a face that was neither beautiful nor unattractive but, as she said herself, 'just ordinary'. Shy as a child, she remained so in adulthood and, old-fashioned in dress and outlook, she struggled to form relationships or even close friendships, and rarely exchanged more than 'Good morning' and 'See you tomorrow' with any of her colleagues. She attended church every Sunday and went on church socials and barbecues from time to time, but most evenings and weekends she spent alone, but for her pet cat, in her one-bed walk-up a few blocks from the school, reading books or marking papers.

She was always the first out of the staff room at the end of recess, ready to greet the children as they returned to the classroom. She lived for them, endlessly patient, kind and caring, nurturing each of them until they moved on to a higher grade. As they grew older, some of those children remembered her with great affection, but others only laughed behind their hands at her frumpy clothes and prim manner.

Grace had read the newspaper reports and seen the TV coverage of each school massacre. They horrified her and troubled her sleep, filling her mind with visions of 'her' children at the mercy of some psychotic killer. The nightmares worsened when the school began 'lockdown drills' designed to prepare teachers and students for an armed attack. When it was the turn of Grace's class, the school PE teacher pretended to be a gunman trying to force his way into the classroom, while Grace, armed with nothing more threatening than a whiteboard marker, stood ready to fight him off as the students, giggling and laughing, made half-hearted attempts to hide in blind spots in their classroom. However, a rectangular room containing nothing but desk, chairs and one small cupboard offered virtually no blind spots and hiding places, and it made Grace sick to think that if someone really did break in and threaten her kids, she would be nothing more than just a helpless spectator or another victim herself, cowering in a corner until shot.

When, prompted by local Republican politicians, the school board circulated information about shooting courses for teachers, she hesitated, but then applied. None of her colleagues knew she was doing so and wouldn't have believed it if they had been told. It was the most out of character thing that she had ever done and although it frightened her a lot - she had never even held a gun before - it also filled her with a sense of pride and more than a little excitement.

At the range where the course - 'Gunfighting 101 for Teachers' - was held, a dusty, fly-blown lot a few miles from the town of Lynchburg, Virginia, she cut an unusual figure among the other teachers. The oldest person there by some years, she was also one of only three women. The other two were younger and more brash and confident, joshing and joking with the men while, as usual, Grace kept herself to herself.

The course supervisor, Rocky Rogers, was a retired state policeman boosting his police pension by running the firing range. He told every class with folksy charm, 'We pride ourselves on our safety record. We've held almost 100 of these courses now, and you know what? Everyone who was alive at the start of the course was alive at the end of it too.'

For entirely understandable reasons, he made no mention of the accidental shootings that had occurred. In the first one, an instructor - no longer employed by Rocky - had shot one of the course participants in the ass while trying to demonstrate a quick draw. In another incident, a teacher had shot himself in the foot when he thrust his handgun into his belt, still with a round in the breech.

The last and most serious accidental shooting occurred when a male teacher balanced his handgun on the side of the urinal while he was relieving himself. It fell to the floor and went off, hitting the man using the next urinal in the thigh. The round severed an artery and the unfortunate victim had come close to bleeding out before Rocky managed to use his belt as a tourniquet, slowing the bleeding enough for the man still to be alive when the ambulance arrived from the neighbouring town a few minutes later. As Rocky remarked to his wife at the end of that trying day 'I can teach them most things, hon, but I sure as heck can't teach them anything about stupidity, they seem to have learned that all by themselves.' That particular teacher had been reported to the police and charged with a Class B Misdemeanour and though he avoided jail time, he was forced to resign from the school where he had been teaching seventh grade for twenty years.

In an attempt to avoid further mishaps, each person on the course was now allocated a 'shooting buddy', whose principal function was to check that their buddy's handgun was safe and unloaded whenever it was not being used for practice on the ranges. Grace's buddy on the course, Brett Kowalski, was a football coach at a bush league high school in West Virginia. He instilled the need for strength, fitness and athleticism in his pupils but, as Grace thought to herself, it was clearly a case of 'Do as I say, not as I do' because, as befitted a man whose diet seemed to be at least 90 per cent junk food, he was as pale, soft and flabby as a Pillsbury doughboy.

When they were introduced to each other, Brett's expression suggested that a mousey, middle-aged woman was not exactly his idea of the perfect shooting buddy, but he soon warmed to her enough to start confiding in her. While they had been waiting in line to complete their registration and pay their $400 fee - 'It's normally twice that,' Rocky assured them, 'but we want to do our bit to help stop any more Columbines and Parklands' - Brett told Grace about his home town in the South. 'Like football and religion, belief in gun-ownership is one of the articles of faith in the Bible Belt farming community where I grew up. But I only got my concealed-carry permit a couple of months ago. I enrolled in this course so I'm good and ready to take out any SOBs - if you'll pardon my French, ma'am - who come busting into my school. I can handle a weapon all right, but I reckon I still need to keep practising till I don't even notice the sound of the gunshots and I can put every round I fire into the spot on an ace of spades.' He paused for breath and gave Grace a critical once-over. 'But you don't look like a regular huntin', shootin' and fishin' kind of gal, if you don't mind me saying so, ma'am, so what's your motivation?'

Grace gave a wan smile. 'I just want to be able to protect my children - the ones I teach, I mean - but I'm praying that I don't freeze in panic if a gunman ever does come through the door.'

Rocky had overheard the exchange. 'Ma'am, that's why everyone is here,' he said, 'and that's exactly what we aim to teach you in the next couple of days.' He raised his voice. 'Y'all ready? Then let's get to it. Okay, as of now there are fourteen US states where teachers can legally carry a gun at school, and another sixteen where they can do so with the permission of their local school board. I'm assuming that y'all teach in one or other of those states and I've got to tell you that we salute your principles and your courage in taking this step to protect the kids you teach. Me and my partner here, name of Brad, who's ex-law enforcement like me, are going to show you folks how to handle those handguns you'll be concealed carrying in your schools.

'Now the Second Amendment is there for a reason: to let us defend ourselves, our families, our friends and our communities against those who wish us harm - plain and simple. Our children are in your care and we parents trust you to keep our kids safe. So it's only right that you teachers have the means to defend them, and if you are going to take a weapon into school, you sure as heck should be trained how to use it…which is where we come in. Now since the whole idea is that no one should know which teachers are carrying weapons, school principals are not permitted to ask you whether you are carrying a weapon on school premises, and there are no official figures on how many are doing so, but our friends at the NRA reckon that it's only around one per cent.'

He let a dramatic pause build before continuing. 'If you're a terrorist or a psychopath, those must look like pretty good odds. So let's see what we can do to even up those odds a little. Now we don't do any training in de-escalation, talk-downs or any of those other fancy things, because all that stuff is supposed to have happened before y'all came here. But let me state for the record that if you can resolve a situation peacefully, then obviously you should, but high school shooters are not usually open to persuasion and if any of you teachers are gonna end up in a gunfight, you need to be able to shoot your way out of it without getting harmed your good selves.

'So ... course content: we'll be covering safety procedures, stripping and assembling, stoppage drills, stances, types of cover and firing. We'll be showing you how to concealed carry your weapon - and concealed carry obviously means out of sight, either on the body or in any kind of container, including a purse. However, be aware that no weapon is ever going to be 100 per cent safe or 100 per cent concealable in a school environment, so your watchword should be vigilance at all times. Now we'd like to spend longer with y'all, but we know time is very important to teachers, so we've designed a course that is high in intensity but of short duration. It's just two days but I guarantee you that by the end of it, you'll be able to carry and use your weapon with total confidence.

'We're often asked what sort of handgun we'd recommend. Well, there is no "one size fits all" answer to that, because your build and strength will dictate the size and weight of the weapon that you can handle but, as I'm sure you know, there are two basic types of handguns: revolvers and semi-automatics. The pros of revolvers are that they have a pretty uncomplicated mechanism and practically never have a stoppage when firing, making them a safer choice for a less knowledgeable user. However the cons are that you're limited to five or six rounds before having to reload. They're known as six-shooters for a reason, but I'd recommend only loading five rounds because the safest way to carry a revolver is with the hammer resting on an empty chamber. If it's resting on a loaded one and you drop the weapon, it may just go "Bang"! A shortage of rounds is not a problem with semi-automatics because they can hold 20 or 30 in the magazine, but the downsides are that they have a complicated mechanism, and are prone to stoppages if they're not maintained correctly.

'As well as deciding what kind of handgun you want to be carrying, you also need to decide what calibre it should be. Well, here in the US of A there's a scale that, while not totally scientific, does claim to predict how likely you are to die if you're hit by different calibre rounds. Top of the list - surprise, surprise

- are .44 Magnum revolvers - you know, like the one Dirty Harry used in the movies. The US Military also use a .45 round in a semi-auto. Either of those will kill you instantly but there is a great danger of collateral damage, by which I mean that the round will not only kill you, but could go straight through you, out the other side and hit someone else as well, which is not exactly ideal in a school situation. However, the same is true of almost any size round; even if it's a much lower calibre, if it hits you in the wrong place, you'll be just as dead. Anyway, we feel the best compromise for your situation is a 9mm. round in a semi-auto pistol, which gives good killing potential without the risk of too much collateral damage, and with enough rounds in the magazine to take care of most situations.

'Now we'll be issuing you with ear-muffs and protective goggles, courtesy of Health and Safety regulations - if those guys had been around a hundred years ago, the West would probably never have been won - but, like it or not, I'm afraid goggles and ear-muffs are mandatory on all commercial firing ranges. Ironic, ain't it? We have to use safety kit to teach people how to shoot and kill!'

There were also a few more downsides to the training that Rocky did not get around to mentioning. The goggles and ear-muffs often induced a sense of detachment in the firer, making the experience of shooting seem unreal and greatly reducing its value as training to prepare for a real-life incident when ear-muffs and goggles were most unlikely to be worn. Working on an outdoor range also meant that the scenarios they staged were completely unlike what the teachers would experience were they ever unfortunate enough to be involved in a real life shooting in school classrooms and corridors, when the sound of gunfire in those confined spaces would reverberate from the walls in a deafening crescendo, rather than being dissipated in the wide open spaces of the range.

Rocky and Brad did what they could, but they were running a commercial organisation and the only reason they or anyone else was willing to provide training was in order to turn a profit. If there was Federal or State funding as well, so much the better, but even so, most of the training they offered consisted of talking rather than shooting, because talk was cheap and rounds cost money.

There was also insufficient available time or facilities to teach realistic scenarios, but during the next two days on the outdoor range, Rocky and Brad did their best to show Grace and the other teachers-turned-pupils how to conceal themselves behind barrels that they pretended would stand in for bookcases - something which few modern classrooms had in any case - and how to dodge gunfire in a classroom and hallway. The long vistas to the distant mountains on the range were nothing like the cramped confines of a hallway or classroom, but as she went through the drills, Grace did her best to try and picture herself in the corridors of her school.

They fired live-rounds at targets arranged in front of a bulldozed mound of dirt that provided a safe backdrop. Bizarrely they were using paper targets of steel-helmeted Nazi stormtroopers that must have gone out of date at the end of the Second World War but were evidently still being produced. They also practised shooting while sitting or crouching behind a desk - a rusting steel table being pressed into use instead of a desk - and how to draw, aim and fire their weapon in one swift movement. At times, it seemed like being inside an arcade video game but, somewhat to her surprise, Grace found herself revelling in every aspect of the course.

Handling the guns proved much less daunting than she was expecting, the sound of firing was also less frightening than she feared and the feeling of satisfaction she got when, after a few haphazard shots, she started to hit the target more regularly was overwhelming. She loved every moment of it and was sorry at the end of the second day when the course was over.

On her way home she thought about going on to join a local gun club and even drove out to take a look at her local one, but one look at the 'good old boys' hanging around outside when she drove up to it, made her change her plans. However, when she returned to school after the summer recess, she was carrying a concealed handgun in her bag. No one at the school knew about it, but if a killer ever did target her school and her class, Grace would now be ready for him.

CHAPTER 5

Spring Break was in full swing and the high school building in a prosperous Washington DC suburb was deserted save for an elderly janitor, watching soap operas on the TV in his basement room. The unwatched CCTV screens behind him, flickering with ghostly, grey and white images of the school and grounds, showed a black-clad figure, wearing a backpack, climbing the perimeter fence and slipping between the pools of shadow to the building.

Shorty had studied the building through binoculars and found what he was seeking on the first floor: a window that, although closed, had been left unlatched. He scaled the wall with effortless skill, levered the window open with the blade of his combat knife, then swung himself over the sill. He paused to close and latch the window, ran his gaze over the ceiling and then eased open the classroom door.

After listing intently for several minutes, and hearing no sound but the faint murmur from the janitor's TV two floors below, Shorty took a chair from the classroom and moved off down the corridor.

Halfway along it, he came to a halt beneath a hatch in the ceiling. He took a plastic sheet from his backpack, spread it beneath the hatch to catch any debris, then placed the chair in the middle and stood on it. He pushed up the hatch, stood on tiptoe on the chair and shone his Maglight torch around the roof void. Using the tip of his knife blade, he bored a narrow hole through the ceiling panel, then pushed his backpack up through the hatch and climbed down.

He returned the chair to the classroom, carefully refolded the plastic sheet and slipped it inside his jacket, then crouched beneath the open hatch and sprang upwards, clamping his outstretched fingers onto the edge of the frame. He hauled himself up as smoothly as if he was doing pull-ups in the gym, crouched down while he replaced the hatch, and pushed an endoscope into the hole he had made. He checked the image from it on his iPhone and adjusted its position slightly so it showed more of the corridor beneath him, then moved past the dusty boxes of old term papers and box files stored in the roof void, and squatted down behind them.

From his backpack he took enough supplies to last at least 48 hours: a couple of packs of army combat rations, a large plastic bottle full of water and an empty one that he would piss into when necessary. Using his backpack as a pillow, he stretched out and closed his eyes. He had a long time to wait.

The school began to come to life again just after dawn on the Monday morning. Two security guards

- both armed as a result of a Congressional decree following the latest in the long line of American high school shootings - this one leaving 27 children dead - made a sweep of the building, checking doors and window-locks. Neither even thought about checking the roof void. One of them then manned the metal detector at the school entrance while the other patrolled the corridors. Both were ex-military, one had served in Iraq, the other in Afghanistan but, confined to guard and general duties, neither had seen combat.

In his dark eyrie above the corridor, Shorty heard the noise of the outside world gradually increase. There was a rising babble of voices as children passed through the security scanner and flooded the corridors, swapping Spring Break stories as they headed for their classrooms, then the strident ringing of the school bell, followed by the sound of closing doors and a sudden silence as the first lessons began. By the light of his torch he studied a photograph of a teenage girl with long blonde hair, etching every detail of her face into his memory. He flicked a lighter, burned the photograph and crumbled the ashes to powder in his gloved fingers.

Wearing a long-sleeved shirt, gloves, a baseball hat and a Donald Trump face-mask, concealing every part of his face and body, Shorty stacked his loaded backpack next to the hatch and studied the endoscope image on his iPhone. He saw the security guard pass beneath him, just as he had every five minutes since he had begun patrolling and as he moved out of sight, Shorty eased up the hatch and silently put it to one side. He pulled the endoscope free from the ceiling and slipped it into his back pack. Five minutes later he watched the guard's return and as he passed below, he dropped though the hatch, landing a couple of feet behind him. In one move he threw himself forward, one arm snaking around the man's neck, while his other hand clamped the guard's weapon to his side. The guard struggled but in vain and the only sound he made was the gurgle in his throat that turned into a death rattle.

Shorty lowered him to the ground and took his weapon from its holster. He pulled the hatch cover back into position then shouldered his backpack and walked down the corridor towards the metal detector where the other guard sat, gazing vacantly out through the entrance doors. He was still staring in that direction when Shorty clamped a hand over his mouth and cut his throat. Shorty held him rigid until his death spasm, then let the body drop. He tucked the dead man's pistol in his belt and was heading back into the school when there was a piercing scream from the upstairs corridor. A child, given permission to go to the bathroom during the lesson, had stumbled on the body of the other security guard.

Showing no sign of stress or haste, Shorty moved along the corridor to the classroom he had chosen. He kicked the door open and put a round into the teacher standing by the whiteboard, his face frozen in panic. As the children began to sob and scream, he identified his target, killed her with a double tap, and then took out a succession of other children as the remainder scrambled for whatever cover they could find beneath the desks. He emptied one magazine, switched to the other weapon and shot two more kids, then turned on his heel and began walking towards the entrance.

A classroom door burst open further down the corridor and Grace ran out, tugging at the pistol in her purse. Shorty almost laughed. He knew that some teachers - and clearly that even included middle-aged women - carried concealed weapons in case of an attack on their schools and had some training in how to use them. That was fine in theory, but a theory was all it was. Faced with the reality: an armed man who had fired his weapon thousands of times in training and many more times in combat, rather than a few practice rounds at a paper target on a range, there would always be a fatal hesitation or too hasty a shot.

He watched as Grace pulled the handgun clear of the purse, and began to raise it towards him, but she never even had the chance to pull the trigger. Still with a half-smile on his face, Shorty put a double-tap into her. The first shot smashed into her sternum, the second, a heartbeat later, blew her brains all over the classroom door she had just opened. She was dead before her body had even hit the floor.

As the screams from the terrified children reached a crescendo, Shorty walked purposefully towards the main doors, putting a final shot through the glass in the school office to discourage any staff there from playing the hero. He tossed the weapon into the pool of congealing blood surrounding the dead security guard by the scanner and strolled out, pulling off his mask as he reached the gates. Within two minutes, just as the first sound of wailing sirens could be heard in the distance, an anonymous-looking saloon pulled out from the kerb where it had been parked for the previous two days and merged into the mid-morning traffic.

CHAPTER 6

Shorty struck twice more over the following months. In both cases the high school was in a well-heeled, largely white suburb, had armed guards and some teachers carrying concealed weapons and who were trained to respond to a shooting. In both cases, Shorty dispossessed the guards of their weapons, shot any teachers who tried to challenge him and killed an apparently random collection of children.

The NRA adopted its usual tactics to each shooting, buttressed by the loyalty of politicians on both sides of the House and Senate, bought with campaign contributions and the tacit threat that those who opposed the NRA would find well-funded candidates standing against them at the next election. Their proposed solutions to the epidemic of school massacres included allowing even more teachers to carry concealed weapons and giving them yet more weapons training, banning video games, installing more facial recognition systems and metal detectors in schools, and using more and more police officers to augment or replace the security guards already

working in schools. The effectiveness of such SROs
- School Resource Officers - was hotly disputed and
a police officer at one school where a massacre had
occurred became a national hate figure after remaining outside the building while the shooter was inside,
killing students with an assault rifle.

Some right-wing Republicans even advocated
banning all media coverage of school massacres,
arguing that the publicity only encouraged more
of them. Despite the killings, as the NRA prepared
for its annual convention in Kansas City, deep in the
American heartlands, its leader was in typically bull-
ish mood.

CHAPTER 7

Richard Yokely climbed out of the cab and looked up at the brick-fronted town house with wrought iron metal balconies. He was in Old Town, Alexandria, the port area of Washington DC since colonial times. He was there to see Senator Rex Adams, a heavy-weight politician and a long-time friend of Yokely's. Born into a wealthy African-American East-Coast family, the Senator had attended an Ivy League university before going to Oxford as a Rhodes Scholar. After graduating he had gone straight into politics, working as an Intern to a Democratic Senator. His career since then had been on an unbroken upward trajectory and he now chaired the National Security Agency Oversight Committee. Yokely had dressed appropriately in a dark blazer, grey trousers and a crisp white shirt, and his trademark black loafers with tassels on them.

The Senator had also become the conduit between the White House and Grey Fox group and Yokely knew that his invitation to the Senator's house was business and not social. Grey Fox was the agency that the President turned to when he had problems that the conventional agencies were unable to deal with. Often those problems could only be resolved by assassination, something that Grey Fox operatives were skilled at. In years past, Yokely would be briefed by the President or the Vice President, often in the White House itself. He had met every president from Ronald Reagan to Barack Obama and had carried out missions for them all. But the current incumbent of the White House had not been told of the existence of Grey Fox, partly over fears that he might mention it during one of his regular late-night Twitter sessions, but also because of the genuine risk that he would want to use the agency for his own ends.

Yokely rubbed the back of his neck. He was dog-tired. It wasn't the fact that he had just gotten off a plane after a five-hour flight from San Diego, it was the three days he'd spent without sleep in Mexico with two undercover DEA agents that had done the damage. They had been on the track of an enforcer for one of the Mexican cartels who had been responsible for a string of high-profile assassinations, including three DEA men. The DEA men hadn't just been killed, they had been tortured and mutilated and videos of the murders had been posted on Facebook. Yokely's mission had been as much about revenge as it had been about taking down a cartel killer, and once they had cornered the man in the bedroom of his villa, they had set about killing him in the same way that he had killed the DEA agents. The cartel had been sent a message that they would ignore at their peril.

He walked up a short flight of steps and made use of a door knocker in the shape of a racing stirrup. The door was opened by a liveried butler who was clearly expecting Yokely and who led him down a carpeted hallway to a study at the back of the house. Half of the room was lined with leather-bound books, the other half was a conservatory with windows overlooking the substantial garden.

The Senator was dressed for the golf course, sporting a canary yellow pullover and checked trousers, but Yokely couldn't tell if he was on the way out to play or had just got back. He was sitting at a two-hundred year old desk on which were two state-of-the-art Apple monitors and he winced as he got to his feet. The man had been injured twice during his military career and both times had been awarded a purple heart. The Senator smiled and held out his hand. 'Good to see you again, Richard.' His hair was unnaturally black, almost certainly dyed, and had a metallic look to it. His skin was smoother than normal for a man in his early seventies, and Yokely figured that he had benefitted from Botox at the very least.

'You too, Senator.'

The two men shook hands and the Senator waved for Yokely to go through to the conservatory where there were two cane-backed sofas either side of a bamboo and glass coffee table. They sat down on separate sofas. The Senator crossed his legs and straightened the creases of his golf trousers. 'You've heard about the school shootings, obviously?' he said.

'Of course,' said Yokely.

'They couldn't have come at a worst time,' said the Senator. 'Our society is more fractured than at any time since the Civil War. The nation is a powder keg, with every section of the population seemingly at war with every other one: white against black, rich against poor, North against South, the Coast against the Centre, Republicans against Democrats, conservatives against liberals, evangelicals against all of them. No one trusts anyone and too many people and organisations seem prepared to take the law into their own hands ... which is exactly what I'm now being forced to do myself to try and keep a lid on it. The longer these attacks continue, the wilder the conspiracy theories and rumours that are going to be circulating. Some black extremist groups are already openly celebrating the killing of rich white children, while the NSA are monitoring communications between groups of white supremacists who are talking about using the attacks as a trigger for a race war. I'll go to any lengths and take any risks to prevent that from happening, but I do not intend to be stupid about it. If it were to be revealed that I had gone behind the backs of our own security services ...' He shrugged. 'You need to keep a low profile, obviously.'

'We always do,' said Yokely. 'But isn't the order coming from the President?'

'The president is still unaware of Grey Fox and hopefully it will stay that way,' said the Senator. 'But he wants this dealt with, obviously.'

'He can't be happy about the masks.' The killer in all three school shootings had been wearing a mask of the President's face. If indeed it was the same shooter. The police still didn't know if it was one man or if there were copycats.

'He thinks that the masks show that it's the Democrats behind the shootings.'

Yokely's eyebrows headed skywards. 'Is he serious?'

'It's hard to know, him being the way he is.' Senator Adams lowered his voice, even though they were alone in the room. 'Let's be clear. I don't want an arrest, because I don't want this going to trial. There's enough friction and division in this country already; we're like a Molotov cocktail just looking for a flame and the longer this perpetrator remains at liberty, the likelier it is that his actions will be the spark. A trial could also bring a lot into the open that I'd sooner stay hidden and might give extremists on both sides a cause they could exploit. So I want this done, quickly and permanently, with no loose ends. I'd prefer it to be done discreetly, but to be frank, if it has to be done during the half-time show at the Super Bowl, so be it. Just make sure you kill him.'

He waited for Yokely's nod of agreement before continuing. 'Now I've told the FBI they have to co-operate with you and your team and share any and all information they have.'

'You realise that criminal investigations aren't really my forte?'

'Regular law enforcement will do the legwork, of course. But I'd like you to take a broader view of the investigation. For instance it seems to me obvious that it's one person behind the killings and that one person almost certainly has a special forces background. And special forces is very much your forte.'

'What do you want me to do, investigation-wise?'

'Whatever needs to be done,' said the Senator. 'The FBI has its best people on the case, obviously. But they don't have your skill set. I've asked one of the special agents on the case to act as your liaison. Neil Lancaster.' He handed a cardboard file to Yokely. 'His number is in there, plus some broad brush info on the three shootings.'

'And how much does this Lancaster know about me?'

'Just that you're working out of the White House. You can trust him. He's destined for greater things.'

CHAPTER 8

Yokely had booked himself a suite at The Jefferson, with a view of the Washington Monument from its balcony. The building was almost a hundred years old and he enjoyed the European feel of the many paintings and sculptures dotted around. He arranged to meet Neil Lancaster for breakfast and the FBI agent was punctual, arriving at the restaurant at precisely eight o'clock.

Lancaster was black and in his mid-thirties, wearing wire-framed spectacles, a very sharp dark blue suit and gleaming black brogues. There had been no information on the agent other than his phone number in the file the senator had given Yokely, but from his appearance and lack of physical presence he guessed the man didn't have a military background.

Over eggs and bacon and pancakes and mugs of coffee, Yokely probed the FBI agent and discovered that he had a law degree and had joined the FBI straight from college. He was from New Orleans but had lost most of the accent, had been a keen football player at university and his father was a postal worker who was close to retirement. Lancaster answered all questions quickly and without any trace of guile, and didn't ask any in return. Yokely waited until their plates were cleared before bringing up the investigation. 'So what do you have so far?' he asked.

'Not much,' said Lancaster. 'We still don't know if this is one shooter or a shooter and one or two copycats.'

'What does the CCTV show in terms of body shape and gait?'

'It looks like a match, yes. But he's above average height, average build, average shoe size. It could be one person, could be two, could be three.'

'Clothing?'

'Different clothing and different shoes every time, but then if he's serious about not getting caught he'd be getting rid of the clothes between shootings.'

'Why do you say that? About him being serious about not getting caught?'

'Spree killers usually end up dead or in custody,' said Lancaster. 'They start shooting and they don't stop until someone stops them. School shooters are usually motivated by anger or vengeance, often kids who feel that the whole world is against them and the shooting is often a prelude to suicide, either killing themselves or getting the cops to do it for them. This killer is different. He's calm and controlled and when he has finished killing, he makes his escape.' He shrugged. 'It's unusual. So far as I know, no other high school shooter has ever carried out more than one attack. Normally the victims are random, killed by an individual with a grudge against the school or its teachers.'

'If it is one killer, could he be a former pupil or teacher with a grudge against all of the schools?'

Lancaster shook his head. 'We checked. There's no single connection between all three, and dozens that connect two. But we checked all those connections and they all have alibis for the times of the shootings.'

Yokely sipped his coffee. 'So you've got nothing?'

'We've got footprints. We've got shell casings. We know how tall he is. We know he's cool under pressure which suggests former military or a former cop.'

'Maybe not former,' said Yokely. 'He could still be serving.'

Lancaster nodded. 'Agreed,' he said. 'We do have one tenuous connection. I'm not sure if it's even worth mentioning.'

'At this stage, anything is up for discussion,' said Yokely.

'It's about the victims,' said Lancaster. 'The shooting appeared random, but in each case one was the child of a very prominent public figure, a Republican governor, a senator and a big city mayor.'

'You're thinking it isn't a coincidence? What if those kids were the real target and the other victims just collateral damage?'

'It sounds crazy, I know.'

'The kids were targeted because they were rich and white? So it's racist? Is there any evidence that the killer is black?'

Lancaster shook his head. 'We don't think it's racist. Some of the other victims were black, others Hispanic. The killer hasn't been targeting white kids specifically, it's just that at each school, there was the child of a prominent person dead. But then the schools were in affluent neighbourhoods, so it's possible it's a coincidence.'

Yokely nodded. 'If he was targeting the kids because of who their parents were, why would he kill the children rather than just going after the senator, the governor and the mayor themselves?'

Lancaster shrugged .'Maybe because the pain is greatest if you're left alive to reflect and grieve on the child you've lost.'

'And maybe that's a pain that the killer also feels?' Yokely said. 'Have you tried looking at relatives of children killed in previous shootings?'

'That hadn't occurred to us,' said Lancaster.

'It's just a thought,' said Yokely. 'Meanwhile, can you take me to the site of the last shooting?'

Lancaster nodded. 'Sure, it's not far away.'

CHAPTER 9

The school was half an hour's drive away. Lancaster had a black Chevy Impala which still had its new car smell. Yokely fancied a cigar but Lancaster didn't have the look of a smoker so he left them in his pocket. Lancaster parked in a visitor's bay close to the main entrance and the two men climbed out. There was the background hum of traffic from the highway and the repetitive noise of jets inbound to Dulles Airport, as they went into the school building.

As they walked along the corridors and paused in turn at the scenes of each of the shootings, Yokely tried to recreate the chain of events leading up to the killings in his mind, imagining what he would have done, had he been planning the attack and carrying it out. They retraced the route the killer must have taken, seeing what he would have seen, doing what he must have done and identifying places where he might have been seen by a witness. Having walked the killer's entire route within the school, they returned to the place where the first victim - the patrolling guard - was killed. Yokely's gaze swept over the floor and the walls, unnaturally clean where the blood spatters had been washed away.

'Why here?' he muttered to himself.

'What do you mean?' asked Lancaster.

'Why was the first guard killed here? And why this one before the guard at the entrance?' As his gaze travelled over the ceiling, he had his answer. 'Have you got any latex gloves?'

Lancaster did, and he handed a pair to Yokely who put them on before easing up the hatch in the ceiling. He balanced on the balls of his feet and sprang upwards, gripping the edge of the frame and hauling himself up. He crouched over the hatch, using the torch on his phone to light the loft space. A thick layer of dust lay over most of it, but the areas around the hatch and behind a pile of boxes and papers were clear of dust, either because something had been dragged across them or because someone had been sitting or lying there. He spotted the small round hole next to the hatch and squatted down to photograph it and minutely examine it. There was a faint notch in the edge of the exposed drywall, where a cord or wire had rubbed against it.

Yokely dropped down. Lancaster was clearly wondering what was going on, but the FBI agent waited for Yokely to speak. 'The killer spent time up there. Maybe several days. You need to get a CSI team up there.'

'So you think the guy didn't enter the school on the day of the killings? He was already here, hiding in the roof-space above the corridor?'

'Exactly.'

'So how did he get past the guard and the security scanner at the entrance?'

'He didn't. My guess is that he broke into the school when they weren't there, at night or more likely over the previous weekend.'

Lancaster frowned. 'But in that case he'd have been there at least 48 hours, so he must have had water and probably food with him, and that means human waste.'

'But he wouldn't have left it there. He'd have taken it with him.'

Lancaster wrinkled his nose in distaste. 'That's gross.'

'It's a standard special forces technique during long term surveillance,' said Yokely

'Sounds like you're speaking from experience.'

'I am,' said Yokely. 'Right, let's go outside, I could do with a cigar.'

CHAPTER 10

The post-rush hour lull was over and Harbor Bridge Boulevard was crowded with shoppers and tourists, the air heavy with the aroma of Baltimore's signature fast food: crab-cakes. A tall figure stepped out of the shadow of a doorway. Shorty was wearing leather gloves and dressed in nondescript dark clothing, but he was marked out by the battered black Homburg hat he was wearing as he strolled along, rolling a plastic toothpick between his lips. He joined the throng of shoppers crowding the entrance to a store and as he went in, he turned and held the door open for the next few people behind him. It was an old-fashioned and unexpected courtesy rarely seen on the streets of Baltimore, and it also seemed somehow out of place with the piercing look he directed at each person who passed him.

Shorty moved on at the same unhurried pace to the cosmetics counter, where he tried a couple of after-shave lotions and adjusted the rake of his hat using one of the multitude of mirrors around the counters. As he did so, only the sharpest of observers would have noticed his keen gaze travelling over the reflections of those standing around and behind him.

He sauntered on through the store and rode the escalator to the first floor. Like most of the other shoppers, he glanced around as it went up, taking in his surroundings. He spent a couple of minutes looking at clothes, but then went back down to the ground floor and left the store through a side-entrance without making a purchase.

He turned the corner and paused at once, his attention apparently caught by something in the window display, though his gaze was directed back through the corner windows. After a few moments he retraced his steps and waited for the lights before heading on around the harbour.

Shorty adjusted his pace so that he reached the street just as the 'Walk' light changed to a flashing 'Don't Walk'. Once more he scanned the faces of those hurrying across with him before the traffic began to move. As anyone trained in surveillance knew, if you make eye contact with someone, you will remember their face even if you cannot remember from where. If he was being tracked, he was burning off the followers one by one.

He crossed another couple of streets in the same way, slowing his pace still more so that any followers would be bunched behind him. He knew that to trail someone along a busy street, the followers had to be almost within touching distance of their target. He strolled along, apparently almost at random, but now heading west out of the city towards Harlem Park. Some areas had been gentrified, with the traditional Baltimore 'row houses' - terraces - neatly painted, but others were blighted by urban decay, with whole streets shuttered and boarded up, or occasionally a still-occupied house, all that was left of a terrace, standing isolated, surrounded by dereliction and demolition.

The houses lining the streets around Lafayette Park were for the most part occupied and well-cared for, but there were few people on the streets and even fewer in the park itself, an oasis of grass and mature trees in the middle of the urban wilderness. The park was deserted, forcing any watchers to drop well back. Shorty picked up speed, walking an apparently aimless course that brought him back out of the park on West Lafayette. Any watchers behind him would now be sprinting to catch up. The street was busy with parents and children making their way home from the elementary and middle school just along the street. As he rounded the corner of the block, out of sight of any pursuers for a moment, he whipped the Homburg from his head and crushed it inside his jacket.

Surveillance teams are trained to recognise and follow a target by his silhouette, his posture and his gait, but the eye and the brain - and sometimes the followers themselves - are lazy. If the eye has a distinctive marker to follow, like a bobbing Homburg, it will do so. Remove the marker and the target beneath it disappears.

Shorty moved on through the crowds of kids and adults, unhurried, adjusting his pace to the people around him, and still following the route he had planned before setting out that morning. After a couple of blocks he pushed the crumpled Homburg into a plastic bag and dropped it in a dumpster on the corner of the street.

For the next hour he moved through the streets, repeating his anti-surveillance and counter-surveillance drills like an Eastern bloc spymaster on the way to meet a contact. Even after all that effort, if he still had the least suspicion that he was being tracked, he would have aborted and walked away without a second thought.

By the time he had made his way to the dingy streets of Sandtown, one of the most blighted areas of the city, where one third of the housing was derelict, he was sure that he was not being followed, but he set one last trap for any pursuers. He made an abrupt turn, cutting through a long, narrow alley between two empty warehouses. At the far end he stopped and looked back. The alley was empty. He moved away across the street, taking a final look back before disappearing into another alleyway.

Shorty turned down a rutted and cratered sidestreet, and crossed another weed-strewn empty lot. Beyond it were a few blocks of boarded-up row houses, dilapidated stores and run-down warehouses, a shabby no man's land far from the cranes piercing the skyline closer to the city centre that marked the slow advance of the front line of urban renewal.

The street was empty of people but still he did not approach his destination directly. It was a warehouse once used by a food importer but now half empty, with a few small businesses renting parts of the space. He circled right around the block, casting a casual glance at a dusty, cobwebbed, ground floor window, protected by rusting steel bars. At last he unlocked the outer door and entered the building. The light-bulb in the dark lobby was broken, trash was piled under the stairs and the acrid stink of urine hung in the air.

The door to his right looked no different from the others opening off the lobby, but it was fitted with four security locks and, though there was no visible sign of it from the outside, the chipped, painted wood had been lined with sheet steel. He pulled a bunch of keys from his pocket and opened the locks in strict sequence – second, fourth, third and first.

As he swung the door open, the light of a passive infra-red motion detector blinked on in the far corner of the room. He shut the door behind him and switched on the harsh neon lighting. Then he crossed the room, his pace still unhurried, though he had only seven seconds. He took the plastic tooth-pick from his mouth and inserted it into the small hole in the bottom of the motion detector. The light winked out at once.

Shorty glanced around him as he took off his leather gloves and replaced them with a pair of surgical gloves. It was a rectangular room about thirty feet by twenty. A blind obscured most of the natural light from the single small window. There was a cracked and chipped sink in one corner and a toilet in another, screened by a wooden partition. The broad shelves lining the two long walls of the room were filled with tools, soldering irons, and radio, electrical and electronic testing equipment. An oscilloscope showed a green visual image of radio waves. There were also boxes of micro-switches and timing devices, a pile of padded envelopes, packs of different-sized batteries, rows of bottles, canisters of household detergents and cleaning chemicals, and a plastic drum of sodium chlorate.

Everything was in neat order and the work surfaces were scrupulously clean. The workbench was covered by a cheap plastic tablecloth with a heavy vice at one end. He took a padded envelope from the shelf and placed it on the workbench then opened the drum of sodium chlorate, measured out an amount and began mixing it with another chemical. When it was mixed to his satisfaction, he poured it into the envelope, mixed it with powdered magnesium from a smaller plastic drum and then fixed a short length of aluminium section in the vice. He worked on it with a file until a mound of silver-grey filings had collected beneath it. These too he mixed with a chemical and added to the envelope.

Shorty had assessed and discarded a number of possible methods of detonation. Micro-switches were effective but traceable and a radio-controlled device could be triggered by the ambient radio waves in a big city, and he had no intention of becoming a victim at this stage of his campaign. Instead he laid out on the tablecloth the equipment he had chosen for the timer: two batteries, a handful of steel wool and a glass phial containing a copper wire under tension from a spring. Then he began to construct the electrical circuit, testing it carefully at each stage.

He built in an anti-handling device, made from a short length of quarter-inch tube, two thumb tacks and a ball bearing. When he tilted the plastic tube, the ball bearing rolled down and bridged the gap between the thumb tacks to complete the circuit. The steel wool began to smolder.

He broke the circuit at once, letting the ball bearing roll back down the tube and then connected the two wires projecting through the envelope; the anti-handling device would only become armed when they were removed.

Finally he primed the timer by filling the phial with liquid from a glass-stoppered bottle. A curl of smoke rose from the copper as the sulphuric acid began to work on it. He pushed in a bung to seal the tube.

Still moving without haste, he added a pint bottle filled with accelerant to the envelope. Petrol would have done just as well, but he used white spirit he'd bought from a paint store. Last of all, he eased the timing circuit into the envelope and then sealed it with parcel tape. He returned his tools to the shelf and carefully folded the tablecloth, then cleaned down the bench with bleach and a handful of rags. The cloth and the rags went into a crumpled carrier bag. Then he stripped off his surgical gloves, replacing them with his leather pair.

Before he added the surgical gloves to the bag, he held them in the flame of a disposable lighter until they were blackened and twisted. They had to be destroyed; forensics could provide identifiable fingerprints from the inside of such gloves. Then he walked out, locking the door behind him and tossing the bag into a dumpster as he walked away down the street.

CHAPTER 11

Later that afternoon, a motorcycle courier pulled up outside a high-end apartment building in Washington DC. A liveried doorman was on duty in the lobby, presiding over the reception desk and hurrying to hold the door for residents and visitors as they came and went.

Still wearing his helmet, Shorty took out his clipboard and a large padded envelope. It looked no different from the thousands of others delivered in the city every day, except for two small wires trailing from the sides. He looked up and down the sidewalk and waited as a white-haired lady, leading a small Yorkshire terrier, walked slowly towards him. As she passed him, he kicked her legs from under her. She fell with a thud, there was the snap of breaking bone and her howls of agony mingled with the frenzied yapping of the dog.

Shorty opened the lobby door and said to the doorman, 'I think one of yours has just fallen down outside.' As the doorman rushed to help, Shorty slipped into the building and took the elevator to the fourth floor, the one below the penthouse suite. He could hear the faint murmur of voices from the penthouse level but the lobby was empty of people and the housekeeper's cupboard opening off it was unlocked. He slipped inside and it was the work of only a few seconds to pull a few items off the shelves - furniture and floor polish, acetone, candles, cloths, toilet rolls and half a dozen aerosols - and arrange them around the padded envelope. He broke the small window in the outer wall with a blow from the handle of a sweeping brush, increasing the air-flow through the room, then, having positioned the padded envelope to his satisfaction, he pulled out the two wires trailing from the side of it, then let himself out and closed the door.

He leaned into the elevator and pushed the buttons to stop it at every floor on the way down, but then took the stairs instead. When he reached the ground floor, he saw that the doorman was still busy with the old lady with the broken leg. He barely glanced up as Shorty hurried past and a moment later his motorbike revved up and roared off down the street.

For a few more moments nothing moved in the housekeeper's cupboard but dust motes stirred by the breeze through the broken window. Then a thin spiral of grey smoke began to drift upwards with them and seconds later the envelope erupted in fierce white and yellow flames.

The acid had eaten through the copper wire, causing the spring to snap back and complete the circuit. Current from the batteries flowed through the steel wool, which immediately glowed white hot and started to burn, igniting the sodium chlorate mixture. The bottle of accelerant exploded, spraying burning white spirit against the walls and shelves. The materials he had piled around the envelope also caught fire at once and within seconds the whole room was ablaze.

Had the building been relatively modern, it would have been fitted with a sprinkler system. However, although it had been extensively refurbished and fitted with modern conveniences including an elevator, the building was a historic one, dating from the 19th century, and exempt from most modern planning regulations. As a result, whether from oversight or cost-cutting, no sprinkler system had been installed and the fire burned unchecked.

When the aerosol cans in the store room began detonating in the heat, the door of the apartment next to the storeroom was flung open and the owner glanced around, trying to locate the source of the noise. Then he heard another bang and saw smoke seeping from under the door. He froze for a second, then rushed across the lobby to the fire extinguisher hanging next to the elevator. He opened the door to the storeroom, jumping back as flames leaped out at him. With fumbling hands, he struggled to remove the safety guard, then had to bang the extinguisher twice against the wall before a jet of water spurted out. To his horror, as the water hit the remnants of the padded envelope, the flames immediately doubled in size and intensity.

A trained fireman might have realised what he was dealing with. Burning magnesium has the extraordinary ability to extract oxygen to fuel its combustion from compounds such as H_2O - water - that would not normally be classed as oxidising agents. For example, water directed on to molten magnesium will not extinguish it. Instead the burning magnesium takes the oxygen from the water to fuel its combustion and the remaining hydrogen in the H_2O is released as hydrogen gas, which in turn then combusts and burns with an even hotter flame. Even if some of the hydrogen fails to combust at once, perhaps because the water has temporarily cooled the flame below the ignition point of the gas, it forms an explosive mixture with the air that can then detonate with savage effect.

Unaware of all this, the man just stared dumbfounded, continuing to pour water onto the rapidly expanding blaze until the extinguisher dribbled to a halt. The fire was now raging out of control and after shouting a hoarse warning, he turned and ran for the stairs, pursued by the flames which had escaped the confines of the storeroom and were racing across the landing, engulfing everything in their path.

By the time the Fire Department's engines reached the scene, the building was an inferno. The apartment owners on the lower floors all escaped, although some were treated for smoke inhalation and minor burns. One occupant on the fourth floor jumped from a window to escape the blaze and survived, albeit at the cost of spinal compression and multiple fractures of both legs. There were also five fatalities: three people trapped on the fourth floor and two in the penthouse were asphyxiated by smoke or burned to death.

CHAPTER 12

The fact that one of the victims of the firebombing - the owner of the penthouse apartment - was a prominent arms manufacturer, a vocal NRA supporter and a very substantial donor to Republican causes, alerted Yokely and Lancaster. Lancaster made a few phone calls and then updated Yokely in the bar of The Jefferson over coffee and club sandwiches.

'The first thing to note,' Lancaster said, 'was the sophistication of the incendiary device that started the blaze. This guy, whoever he is, is smart. As fuel and accelerants, he made use of the sort of household chemicals and materials you'd find in any house or apartment block, but the device itself contained powdered magnesium and aluminium and, as you know, they are particularly dangerous, because any attempt to extinguish them with water merely fuels the flames. The means he used to gain entry to the building was brutal. He tripped up an old lady, breaking her leg in the process and while the doorman was distracted, the perp entered the building, took the lift to the floor below the penthouse, where the arms manufacturer lived, set the device in the house-keeper's store room and then made his getaway while the doorman was still tending the injured woman.'

'Any CCTV?' asked Yokely.

Lancaster shook his head. 'There was CCTV, but the perp was posing as a motorcycle courier and was wearing leathers and gloves with a helmet and visor completely obscuring his face. So, surprise, surprise, police and fire investigators have no clues to go on.' He paused. 'Now here's the really interesting bit. The police received a number of bomb warnings before the incident. Nearly all of them were made from untraceable burner phones or telephone-booths and there's no apparent geographical pattern to them. The only quirk I can see is that the initial calls were made not to 911, but to local police precinct houses. But I also listened to the recordings of the bomb warnings and the voices of the callers are significant. The FBI tech guys have spliced the police tapes together.' He pressed a button on his smartphone and then held it out. Yokely took it and put it to his ear and listened as a metallic-sounding recorded voice began delivering its chilling message. 'Shut up and listen. There's a bomb in a building on Connecticut Avenue, timed to go off in sixty minutes.'

There was a brief silence, then another warning. 'There's a bomb near North Capitol Street.' There was a clunk, followed by the dial tone as the caller hung up.

Yokely gave the phone back to Lancaster.

'As you'd expect, those hoax warning calls caused all sorts of chaos, forcing police into time-consuming, fruitless searches and the evacuation of buildings in heavily populated areas, while taking police and fire crews away from the area where the fire-bombing actually took place,' said Lancaster. 'What did you notice about the voices?'

Yokely shrugged. 'They were male but heavily distorted.'

'They're synthesiser-generated. Untraceable.' Lancaster gave a weary shake of his head. 'None of the police department personnel who received the calls thought that significant enough to mention. Now listen to the next few.' He tapped the screen again and gave the phone back to Yokely.

A variety of male and female voices, speaking with a range of accents, delivered more bomb threats.

Yokely listened and then nodded.

'Those calls were all made to 911 from downtown DC,' said Lancaster. 'There's no electronic distortion, they're obviously different people, and almost all are specific of a particular business or office. What we have there is workers beginning to see hoax bomb threats as a way of prolonging their lunch-breaks or finishing early for the day. Now listen to the last call; the one that came true.'

He tapped the screen again and Yokely put the phone to his ear. He felt the hairs rise on the back of his neck as he listened again to the disembodied, synthesised voice. 'There's a fire bomb on 16th Street, Downtown. Timed to go off in ten minutes.'

Yokely nodded. 'So he gave a warning,' he said, 'but nowhere near enough time to allow sufficient time for police to do anything about it, so either he was trying to salve his conscience a little or, more likely maybe, he was just toying with the cops.' He rubbed his chin. 'We're looking for a professional of a very specific kind.'

Lancaster gave him a puzzled look. 'What do you mean?'

'It's a classic special forces approach: where possible make use of materials that are available on site or nearby, keep it simple - don't make your device any more complex than it needs to be - use a timer or other device to give you distance from the target, and spread as much disinformation and sow as much confusion among the opposition as you can.'

'So what are you saying?'

'I'm saying that if this guy isn't a special forces soldier, he's giving a very good impression of being one.'

CHAPTER 13

The buck raised its head, warily scenting the dawn breeze as its harem of does grazed, unconcerned. Nothing moved among the pines or on the steep rock walls of the glen and the only sound was the soft tearing of the mountain grasses as the deer browsed among the trees.

The line of the watery sunrise inched its way down the rockface, while overhead an eagle launched itself from the crags, its outline stark against the cloudless sky. Pricked by his instinct but unable to find any source of danger, the buck remained motionless for some time, but at last lowered his head and began to graze again.

Suddenly one of the does dropped to the ground. Her hooves thrashed the air as she writhed in her death throes, her blood mingling with the dew soaking the grass. There had been no gunshot and in their confusion, the remaining deer turned first one way then another, poised on the verge of flight, nostrils flaring, ears twitching, alert for the least sound or movement, or the faintest scent.

The dying doe kicked once more and lay still. Flies began to settle on her staring eyes. As the silence grew, the other deer gradually calmed and at length they began to graze again, apparently oblivious to the dead body in their midst. Then the buck crumpled and fell, blood gushing from a hole in his chest. The does froze for a moment, then crashed away through the underbrush, finally aware that a new, silent death was lurking in the forest.

As the sounds of their panic-stricken flight faded, there was a stirring in a low clump of undergrowth and forest litter at the edge of the clearing, and a rangy figure stood up. His eyes were never still, constantly scanning the forest around him. Shorty wore a shapeless, netting suit, like a shroud to bury the dead, but woven from jute thread, and so studded with dun-coloured rags, torn strips of sackcloth, grasses, leaves and twigs, that it had been indistinguishable from the forest floor.

He removed the netting suit, revealing his worn and faded clothing - jacket, wool shirt and trousers in drab greens and browns, and boots with soft leather uppers and rubber soles - then stretched, easing the stiffness from his cramped muscles. He had lain there throughout the night and the form of his body was imprinted in the flattened grass, a drier, darker shape against the surrounding, dew-silvered vegetation.

Shorty had reached the clearing just before sunset the previous evening, scanning the ground for the spoor of deer and the signs of grazing - cropped grass, bushes stunted by browsing, and moss and lichen stripped from the rocks. He walked on through the clearing, then began to circle back on his own track. After a moment he stopped, smiling to himself at a habit that had become instinctive, even when there was no need for it.

He checked the wind direction, though it could easily shift during the night, and then tried three or four different lying-up places around the clearing, stretching out in each one and sighting through the telescopic sight of his rifle. Finally he found the right place.

He used the last of the light to complete his camouflage and then lay down on his stomach, his gloved hand on the stock of the rifle, his forehead resting on the ground. He closed his eyes and lay motionless, slowing his breathing, aiming for a semi-comatose state in which his metabolism would slow and his body cool. The only sense that remained at full alert was his hearing, so supersensitive that he could detect pine cones falling in the forest a hundred yards away.

Shorty remained there all night, never varying his position, raising his metabolism only when he became too cold or sleep threatened to overcome him. Whenever he felt himself becoming drowsy, he opened his eyes and concentrated on the things directly in front of him - fallen leaves, pine needles, a fallen twig - and forced his mind to work, forming a mental picture of every stage in the development of the object he was staring at. When he was alert once more, he closed his eyes and retuned his ears to the sounds of the night forest.

He knew that if he became too cold, he would begin to shiver uncontrollably, giving himself away, and each time the cold sank deep into his bones, he began a series of minimal exercises. He braced his toes against the soles of his boot, then worked his ankles against the joint and carried on up his body, through the calves, thighs and stomach. He tensed his arms, shoulders, neck and jaw, then inhaled and exhaled rapidly to warm his upper body.

As soon as he began to feel warm, he stopped the exercises and took long, slow deep breaths to re-oxygenate his brain. Then he allowed his metabolism to slow once more. He repeated the cycle throughout the night, increasing its frequency as the cold deepened and frost bit into the glen.

He timed his intervals of exercise so that as dawn approached, his metabolism was so low and his body so cool that frost formed over him, sealing in his scent and making the wind direction of little importance. As day broke, he heard the first faint sounds of the deer approaching through the forest. He lay still, waiting until they settled and began to graze. Then he opened his eyes and sighted through the telescopic sight. He had chosen his lying-up place well; he had to swing the barrel of his rifle through no more than a degree to bring the first deer into his sights.

Shorty stretched his cramped muscles again, but remained in the shadows at the edge of the clearing as his gaze travelled slowly up the glen, alert for any sound or movement - the cry of a bird, the flight of a startled animal through the brush - that would give warning of another human intruder in the heart of the forest. There was nothing but the gentle soughing of the breeze through the branches high above him, and the muffled sound of tumbling water from a distant stream.

He stepped into the sunlight and stood for a moment, letting it warm his body. He was unshaven and his stubble, like his close-cropped hair, was stippled with grey. There was the faint puckered outline of a small scar on his cheekbone.

As he drank some water from his canteen, he felt the pangs of hunger, but food would wait; he had work to do. He crossed to the far side of the clearing and began to drag the deer carcasses down the slope to the floor of the glen. It formed a natural, rock-walled amphitheatre, deep in the heart of the mountains. It had taken him a week to find this place, first studying the contours of likely areas on the maps and then trekking through the mountains to reach them.

Shorty studied a sketch map in his pocket, then began marking off a section of the glen floor, pacing out the distances and using pegs and marker tape to lay out a grid in the dust. In his mind's eye, he could see an emerging pattern: platform, walkways, banked seating, balconies, doors and windows, while the sheer rock-faces rising around him replicated the concrete walls of a huge auditorium.

In the middle of an open area at the far end of the grid, he lashed together three stout branches to form a tripod and propped one of the deer carcasses upright against it. He built a wall of logs and deadfall branches behind it to catch any overshoots. When he had finished he would burn the logs. The only evidence then that anyone had ever been there would be the scorched earth and ashes, and the decaying skeletons of the deer.

He wiped the sweat from his eyes and stood for several minutes, listening intently as his gaze travelled around the deserted rim of the glen. The sun was now high in the sky. As its warmth penetrated deeper among the trees, there was a soft, steady rain of yellowing larch needles and he heard the faint ticking sound as pine-cones opened, firing their seeds in falling arcs over the forest floor.

Shorty saw and heard no human trace and satisfied, he walked over to the rock wall, counting his paces. He stood with his back to the rock and studied the target through the telescopic sight on his rifle. It was a special sniper rifle, so new and secret at the outbreak of the Afghan conflict that even elite combat troops had never been issued with it. It fired high-velocity bullets that could kill at a range of up to a mile but by sacrificing some of that range and using rounds with a lower charge, it was possible to mask the noise of each shot so well that it was almost undetectable from a few yards away.

He slung his rifle over his shoulder and began to climb the side of the glen, feeling the coarse, gritty texture of the rock under his fingers as he tested each handhold before committing his weight to it. He stopped climbing at a broad ledge about fifty feet above the ground. He looked down towards the deer carcass and, knowing that firing downwards makes a target appear closer, he made a mental allowance for that. Then he took a box from his pocket next to him and laid out eight neat rows of rifle rounds. Each was colour-coded with a dab of a different wax crayon.

Shorty took a last glance around the glen, then settled himself into a firing position. He selected a round from the first group and loaded it into his rifle. He used the iron sights on the rifle to aim; they were sufficient for now. When he had finished the tests, he would balance the rifle and zero the telescopic sights. Then everything would be in place.

The deer carcass jumped as he fired the first round into it. There was no crack of fire, no answering echo from the walls of the canyon. The only noise was a 'Phtttt' like a champagne cork being eased from a bottle, barely noticeable among the sound of the breeze rustling the sparse shrubs that struggled for a foothold among the crags.

He laid down his rifle, climbed down and walked over to the target. He examined the small puncture of the entry wound in the deer hide, then cut it open with a hunting knife to check the shock wave that the tumbling bullet-head had made through the flesh, displacing blood and tissue before culminating in a large, jagged exit wound.

The next couple of hours was a tedious succession of aiming, firing, climbing down to check the target, then climbing back up for the next shot, trading-off the noise generated by each different round against the range and power it produced. He paused only to drag the mangled corpse of the first deer from the tripod and replace it with the other one.

At last he was happy that he had the right balance between noise and lethal impact. He fired a final group of five shots with his chosen rounds and put the last shot of all into the deer's head. He knew it had to be a head shot when he came to do the job itself; he would only get one chance, one shot, and it had to be a fatal one. None of the five shots had made much more noise than the sound of a murmured conversation. It would pass unnoticed from a few yards even in a library reading room, let alone in the heart of a busy convention.

Shorty climbed down and walked over to the target to check the impacts. All five shots had torn a bloody trail through the deer's body. The last one had drilled a neat hole through the skull, then blasted out through the back of the head, leaving a mess of blood and brains spattered over the pile of logs.

He returned to the ledge and began balancing and zeroing the rifle. He pulled a scuffed leather case from his inside pocket and took out a set of tiny screwdrivers. Like all armourer's tools, they were wood-handled and brass-tipped - iron or steel tips could strike a spark that might trigger a fatal explosion. He stripped the compensator from the end of the barrel and began the dull but exacting job of adding and removing small weights. He would use no tripod - just more equipment to carry and conceal - but when his work on the compensator was complete, the rifle was so perfectly balanced that it did not jump even a fraction when fired, but only recoiled smoothly into his shoulder.

He then zeroed the telescopic sight: taking it all back to nothing, firing a shot, working the scope to where the round had struck and firing another, until he could put the next shot so close to the one before that the entry wounds merged into one.

Satisfied at last, Shorty collected every spent cartridge from the ledge, then climbed down for the last time. He pulled the carcasses to one side and built a bonfire from his stack of logs, the dry wood giving virtually no smoke as it blazed. He packed away his equipment as the fire settled down, then put some water on to boil for a mug of coffee and sliced a thick steak from the rump of one of the deer with his hunting knife. He impaled it on a sharpened stick and grilled it over the fire.

When he had eaten, he built up the fire again with more deadfalls and logs, then dragged both carcasses over. He crudely butchered them and dumped the pieces onto the pyre, then moved back to the edge of the trees, away from the stench of singeing hair and burning horn. He watched and waited in the cool of the evening air as the fire burned itself out. Then he hid himself among the undergrowth and lay down to sleep.

Shorty woke before dawn the next morning and raked through the still-warm ashes until he had retrieved every spent bullet-head. He kicked the ashes away, threw the remaining deer bones into the stream and scattered armfuls of twigs and forest litter over the fire-site. The next shower of rain - never far away in these mist- and rain-shrouded mountains - would erase any remaining traces of his stay there.

He took a last look around the clearing and then, as the dawn streaked the eastern sky with red, he climbed out of the glen and began heading south, towards the far-distant city. Now at last he was ready.

CHAPTER 14

It was a quarter to ten in the morning but rush hour traffic was still clogging the streets, backed up for twenty blocks. Even the cross-streets were jammed by commuters trying to work their way around the hold-ups. A solitary man, pulling a wheeled suitcase, hurried past the people talking on the street corners and packing the square and disappeared into one of the shabby tenements facing it. The majority of the crowd were men, some no more than 30, others as much as 75 or 80 years old. They stood erect like the military men they had once been, with their campaign ribbons and medals pinned to their jackets, and an assortment of military hats and caps on their heads. They were facing towards the north side of the square, where a group of men stood on the steps of the church, underneath banners inscribed: 'Salute To Our Heroes'. A dozen uniformed soldiers were lined up along the bottom step, standing at parade ground attention as they faced the crowd. To their left, a small but vociferous group held hand-lettered banners reading 'Untie Our Hands' and 'Gun Owners for Peace and Freedom'.

The Reverend Joseph Martin began to address the crowd, stretching his short, squat frame to speak into the microphone. 'Friends, today was to have been a day of celebration of the achievements of black soldiers. But events have conspired to make it also a day of mourning. Jimmy Johnson was shot yesterday morning. Well he wasn't no saint, but he wasn't no devil neither. He had some problems and he was down on his luck, but he didn't deserve to die.'

The crowd responded audibly to his words. 'That's right. Tell it, Reverend.'

'Well we're here to celebrate men of colour who fought for this country; and they fought in every war from the Civil War on, and they are still out there fighting and dying today for this country. But I tell you what, that ain't the only battle people of colour have to fight in these United States and we're getting mighty tired of still having to fight for the freedoms our forefathers were dying for in the Civil War. Will the fight never end?'

There was a roar from the crowd and he mopped his face with a brightly-coloured handkerchief as he waited for the noise to abate. 'Now I know that had Jimmy been spared, he would have been right here, shoulder to shoulder with you men today. He was a veteran too and I know how proud he was to have served alongside, and counted himself a friend of the man standing beside me today.'

He inclined his head towards the well-groomed, grey-haired figure next to him. No army tailor had made the beautifully cut and immaculately pressed uniform carrying the badges of rank of a three-star general.

The Reverend Martin turned back to his audience. 'I knew him too as a child of these streets; I honour him as a man who has shown what talent and determination can do, no matter what obstacles are put in your way. He's a true American hero, and he's a black American hero. And some say he could yet be the next black American President: General Luther Jackson.'

There was a burst of applause as Jackson shook hands with the Reverend Martin and stepped forward to the microphone. Despite the military precision of his bearing, he carried himself with an easy grace, the loose-limbed, balanced walk of an athlete or a boxer. To some African-Americans he really was a hero, but to others, more radical in their views, he was nothing but a 'coconut' - black on the outside, but white on the inside - an Uncle Tom whose rise had largely been achieved through his servility to his white masters. That rise, those critics believed, mocked the vast number of his fellow African-Americans who, however hard they tried, would never be able to achieve a thousandth part of the success, influence and acceptance white society had granted him.

He acknowledged the applause and when it faded, he let a moment or two of silence elapse before he spoke. 'I'm proud to be here today to commemorate and celebrate the role that black soldiers played in shaping our country and fighting for the values we uphold. But I've also come to honour a fallen comrade. Now I can't comment on the circumstances in which Jimmy Jones met his end-' He raised his voice to speak over the swelling rumble of protest. 'I can't prejudge it; there has been no inquiry, no arrest, no charges, and no jury has returned a verdict. But I'll tell you this. I knew Jimmy Johnson. We grew up in these streets together, we enlisted together and we served together. But that's when our paths diverged. When he left the service, like so many other vets, he found himself back in a society that apparently had no use for him. He was a decent, God-fearing, hard-working family man, but back then a vet got no respect from anybody. White vets were ignored and that tells you all you need to know about what happened to black vets.'

He paused for a couple of seconds, his eyes sweeping the crowd. 'Jimmy struggled to adjust to civilian life again, to hold down regular work and keep his family together. He made a few mistakes, like we all do, and things began to go downhill for him. He had a lot to offer, but no one wanted to know and with every passing year, he drifted a little more. Some people said he was an alcoholic, a drug user, a crackhead. Well I don't know about that, but I tell you, that's not the Jimmy Johnson I knew. I knew a man who was a strong and brave fighter, and a talented man. But for reasons that were by no means all his own fault, he turned his back on that talent and his problems ground him down until there was no fight left in him.'

There were grumblings from parts of the crowd and he raised his hands to quieten them. 'Now it's too late for Jimmy; he's dead and gone. But it's not too late for the rest of us to learn the lessons of his life and his unhappy, untimely death. You see, Jimmy's experience is far from unique. And I'm not talking about the manner of his death here, but the course of his life. Like the Reverend here said, our people have fought in every war from the Civil War to Iraq and Afghanistan, but our contribution has never been properly acknowledged. When the battle was hottest, when the shells were exploding and the bullets flying, that's where black soldiers were sent to fight and die for their country. But when there were medals to be handed out, or promotions or jobs as staff officers in Washington to be won, African-American soldiers were at the back of the line. Even a few years ago, the idea of a black general would have been as preposterous as a black President.'

He paused, looking around the sea of faces, confident now of his hold on his audience. 'That's our history, but that's exactly what it is: history, because I'm standing here before you, a black Air Force General, to tell you that anything is possible for African-American people in this country.'

There was another rumble from the demonstrators and he held up a hand. 'I'm not saying racism's dead, far from it. I may be a general, but heck, I ain't that dumb.' He won a burst of laughter from the crowd. 'But I am saying that a black man or a black woman can succeed. Of course it's easier for a WASP with the right connections, the right college background, but it can be done by anyone. I was born and raised no more than a quarter of a mile from here. My story could be yours too.'

CHAPTER 15

General Jackson's amplified voice and the shouts and noise of the crowd carried to an open upstairs window in one of the brownstone tenements facing the square. Invisible to anyone down below a figure stood in the shadows a couple of yards back from the window. The colour of his face was hidden by a ski mask and he stood among a tangle of roughly torn strips of black cartridge paper hanging from the ceiling.

Shorty wore surgical gloves both to hide his fingerprints and to defeat any police paraffin test for gunpowder residue. He fed a single round into the breech of his sniper rifle and laid its long barrel, ending in the snub shape of a compensator, across the forearm he was resting on a chair-back.

As he surveyed the group surrounding General Jackson, he took three deep breaths. He felt the pressure on his diaphragm as his lungs expanded, flooding his body and brain with oxygen. Then he settled himself behind the scope of the rifle. It gave a 45-degree field of vision and was set on the lowest

magnification, twice life-size. He could see the whole
of the group around the General, their mouths opening and closing soundlessly as they chorused their
agreement to his words.

He began to increase the magnification, slowly
eliminating the surrounding men until only Jackson
remained visible, centred in the scope. He paused,
taking a long, almost leisurely look at his target, then
wound up the magnification until all he could see
was an eye and part of the nose, so close it looked to
be right at the end of the scope.

Shorty exhaled slowly as he took up the first pressure on the trigger with his forefinger and, just as he
finished emptying his lungs of air, he squeezed the
trigger. There was a dull sound like the closing of a
refrigerator door, and the eye disappeared from the
scope. In its place was a mist of fine red droplets.

Shorty stood up and began disassembling the
rifle, his movements slow and practised. He removed
the magazine and worked the bolt, extracting the
spent cartridge case from the breech. The butt came
next, then the barrel and the sight, each part fitting
snugly into recesses cut into the foam rubber lining
the suitcase.

He tore down the black cartridge paper and
dumped it in the trash. Finally he removed the surgical gloves, put on a pair of leather ones and then
burned the surgical gloves in the flame of a disposable lighter, until nothing remained but blackened,
twisted husks. No DNA or fingerprints would ever be

obtained from them now. He dropped them in the trash, snapped the case shut and walked out of the door and down the stairs.

There had been no audible gunshot and for a few moments confusion reigned in the square. Then the trail of blood down the steps told its own story. General Jackson lay dead, shot through the eye.

The soldiers lined up along the bottom step stood frozen in indecision. Their rifles weren't even loaded; they weren't issued with ammunition for this kind of duty. Some of the onlookers had drawn their guns, however, and were searching the square, their heads snapping from side to side as they sought a target. They had the scent of blood and death in their nostrils but unlike the deer in the forest they did not flee; they wanted revenge and almost any target would do.

A white, scruffily dressed man who had been walking through the square with his black companion, froze as a voice shouted, 'There he is! That's the cracker bastard!'

Others took up the shout, pointing towards him.

'It wasn't me,' he said, his voice cracking with fear as he spread his empty hands. 'I didn't shoot him.'

It didn't matter. He was white and in the wrong place at the wrong time. There was the rattle of shots, popping and crackling like a brushwood fire. The first three missed their target. One drilled a hole through the windscreen of a stationary truck, the others smashed chips of concrete from the façade of a building and ricocheted away.

The man still stood open-mouthed, rooted to the spot. The next shot hit him in the shoulder, hurling him backwards and spinning him around. As he staggered, his arm hanging useless at his side, two more shots hit him in the back, punching jagged exit holes out through his chest. Fibres torn from his jacket by the impacts blew away like thistledown on the wind. He crashed to the ground, twitched and lay still.

There was more gunfire as the crowd spilled out of the square, while a hundred yards away, a tall figure pulling a wheeled airline suitcase disappeared into the subway entrance. More shots rang out, blacks and whites exchanging fire. There was the crash of breaking glass and the squeal of metal as gates were forced and shops looted.

The traffic remained near-gridlocked. Drivers made desperate attempts to escape, then abandoned their cars and ran. Several were beaten and their cars torched. Columns of black smoke began to rise from the streets as the first red flashing lights cast their glow and the wailing sound of sirens grew ever louder.

CHAPTER 16

It was cold but clear and autumn sunlight was streaming through the windows of the conference room high above the city streets. Senator Adams filled a cup from the water cooler and drank staring down on the traffic crawling past, then, flanked by his aides, he sat with his back to the light, at the centre of one side of the huge oval table. A dozen other people took their seats on either side of him, some wearing suits, others in police or military uniforms.

The Senator ran his fingers through his unnaturally black hair, then glanced at his watch. 'Where the hell are they?'

The Chief of Police, Tom Bradshaw, looked up. His pouched face had the permanently suspicious expression of a bloodhound scratching for a flea. 'It's the traffic. It's been locked solid all morning. Anyways, I don't know why we bother waiting for them, those damn college boys haven't come up with anything so far and there's no reason to think that's going to change anytime soon.'

Senator Adams raised an eyebrow. 'Your own department isn't doing any better, Tom, and anyway, you know as well as I do that you don't have a choice about it. Terrorism and organised crime are both within the Bureau's jurisdiction and-'

'Don't we know it,' Bradshaw interrupted. 'They've been looking over our shoulders ever since 9/11.'

'-and we need their input, because if we don't take this terrorist off the streets fast, the press'll crucify me ... and the FBI will help them do it.'

'We won't let you down, Senator.'

'I'm sure you won't, Tom, but even if you do, it won't be you being nailed to the woodwork, now will it?' As he saw a scowl forming on the police chief's face, he adopted a friendlier tone. 'Anyway, remember what LBJ said? I'd rather have them inside the tent pissing out ...'

He broke off and rose to his feet with a politician's professional smile as the door opened and another group of people was ushered in. He hid another smile as they took their seats on the other side of the table. As usual, they looked about as comfortable in these surroundings as a Baptist convention in a lap-dancing club.

Cameron Murray, the Director of the FBI's Washington office, took the seat facing the Senator. He was sleek, tanned, expensively dressed and slightly overweight, and could easily have been a corporate lawyer. He smiled frequently, but his eyes remained cold and calculating. The Senator had formed an instinctive dislike for him the first time he had laid eyes on him and nothing he had seen in the intervening months had persuaded him to change his opinion.

The Senator's gaze travelled along the row of other FBI faces, familiar from previous meetings. A couple were scowling, crew-cutted throwbacks to the Hoover era, the rest clean-cut college types. All were dressed in sharp, tailored suits with Brooks Brothers shirts and coordinated ties. Even their hair was a cut above that of the men facing them.

The cops were older, more blue collar and more cynical, hard-boiled and hard-bitten. The simmering resentment in the looks they directed across the conference table showed the gulf in background, beliefs and methodology that separated them from the FBI men.

Alongside the senior officers, both the FBI and DCPD teams contained experts - some self-proclaimed, some well-qualified through training and experience - in narcotics trafficking, terrorism, organised crime, smuggling, money laundering, computer hacking and industrial espionage. The Director of the NSA and a CIA liaison officer were also there to act as observers and offer their input if required.

'Well, if we're all here?' The Senator broke off as the door banged again and a slim figure hurried in, wearing motorbike leathers and carrying a black helmet. Murray's eyes flickered over her body as she took off her jacket and dumped it with the helmet on a side table. As she turned round, she intercepted his gaze and her expression contained a hint of distaste, as she sat down with the FBI team.

Senator Adams cleared his throat. 'Director Murray, did you want to introduce your colleague?'

'Sure,' Murray said. 'For those of you who haven't had the pleasure of meeting her yet, this is Ms Greta Durban, a psychologist who is taking over as Criminal Profiler from Al Hoerner.' Murray glanced along the rank of cops facing him. 'Feel free to call her at any time; I'm sure you'll find her every bit as helpful and informative as Al.'

A couple of the cops exchanged glances and rolled their eyes. Hoerner had been so close-mouthed that they'd nicknamed him 'The Clam'.

'As I'm sure you all know,' the Senator said, 'this Task Force was set up with the specific aim of coordinating an effective response to the threat posed to us all by terrorism. And I repeat what I said at our inaugural meeting, it's in everybody's interest to build bridges between all of your organisations. The DCPD and the FBI have fought plenty - too many - turf wars for jurisdiction over previous cases to regard each other as best friends. But I will tolerate no politicking or divisiveness from your men, Chief Bradshaw.' He aimed another smile at Murray, facing him across the table. 'And I expect none from yours.'

'I'd like to reassure the Senator, as I also did at the inaugural meeting,' Murray said, addressing the room at large, 'that our only interest is in solving and preventing crime. There are no egos in need of a massage on this side of the table.'

Tom Bradshaw's lips whitened and he interrupted at once. 'There are no egos on this side either. Just an interest in ensuring that the truth is told and that credit is given where it is due.'

There was a rumble of support from the police officers around him and Murray inclined his head in acknowledgement.

Despite the exchange of platitudes, Senator Adams had no illusions. In such an atmosphere of mutual distrust, no worthwhile information or potential leads would ever be willingly shared.

The two sides began a grudging exchange of information about current operations and intel on future threats. Bradshaw gave a brief summary of the DCPD's current investigations and Murray then replied for the FBI.

When they'd finished, Senator Adams put away his pen and closed his notebook. He had written nothing in it, but then there was little on offer from either side that could not have been culled from the internet or the columns of the Washington Post. 'Well, that's all very interesting,' he said, 'but as I'm sure you must know, there is only one investigation that concerns me right now, and that is the search for the man who has murdered scores of schoolchildren and - if it is the same perpetrator - has also firebombed an apartment building and now shot General Jackson.'

'We've carried out a preliminary evaluation of the evidence gathered from the scene of the crime,' Murray said.

'And? What have you got?' the Senator said. 'And Jesus, I hope it's plenty. The press and the White House have been chewing my balls off every day this week.'

'Intelligence reports and computer sweeps of communication intercepts have again failed to unearth any unusual activity,' Murray said, looking to the NSA Director for support. 'We're cracking down on known extremist individuals or groupings from here to the West Coast, but-'

He glanced at the Senator, whose face betrayed his impatience. 'But we can't just bust heads and arrest people at random, without provoking more attacks and probably riots. If the perpetrator was operating as part of a group, we'd be getting some kind of Intelligence by now - communications intercepts from the NSA, tip-offs from informants, the absence of terrorist suspects from their usual haunts, and so on. The fact that there's a complete Intelligence black hole suggests to me that we're looking for a perp who is not connected to any known terrorist grouping.' He glanced to his right. 'Greta?

'Well, I've not been given a whole lot to go on,' she said. 'But my opinion is that the perp's a loner and a white male ... if only because 95 per cent of psychopaths, serial killers and lone bombers turn out to be white male loners. So that's what he is, or is now, at any rate.'

The Senator's gaze locked with hers. 'Meaning?'

'In my opinion, he's not just some bum with a grudge against authority. The way the attacks have been choreographed and the way that he's upping the ante and increasing the impact, make me think that he's someone who's very methodical, intelligent, organised and disciplined. He's probably had a role in a corporation or other large organisation, and maybe he has a police or military background. If so, something has happened to turn him against everything he once believed in. There must be some personal or private element tied up in it, but I can't see anything among the physical evidence or the pattern of the attacks that would give us a pointer as to what that might be.'

'So ...' Murray said, 'in the absence of any organisation claiming responsibility for the killing, and I know I speak for Tom Bradshaw and his men here as well as the FBI.' His look challenged Bradshaw to disagree. 'Our best guess is that the assassination of General Jackson was the opportunist action of a deranged individual trying to stir up racial conflict, or a group of hitherto unknown political extremists - the Weathermen for the 21st century.'

'Jesus H Christ,' the Senator said. 'Is that it?'

Murray spread his hands. 'Senator, nothing would give me greater pleasure than to have you announce the perp's name, address and description, on the primetime news tonight, but we all have to be patient. Despite the expertise we can draw on and the resources we can bring to bear - and believe me you've got some of the best police brains in the whole United States within this room - we have to be realistic. We're almost certainly looking for someone with no previous criminal record and we have remarkably little physical evidence to go on. We'll nail him, don't doubt that for a moment, but we're in this for the long haul.'

'And that's what the best police brains in the whole United States have come up with?' Senator Adams' voice cut through the room. 'Well you know what? I don't want to hear any more excuses and lame-ass theories. I want facts and results and what I want most of all is to be able to stand up and tell the American public that the perpetrators are dead or behind bars. And I don't give a rat's ass whether it's the FBI, the DCPD, Delta Force or fucking Superman that puts them there.

'Pool the information you have, then get to work. I want every databank searched, every informant squeezed for everything he knows, every rumour followed up. I'm available 24 hours a day if there are developments. Failing that we'll reconvene in seven days to review progress.' He raised his voice. 'And I expect there to be plenty. Those unexplained, unsolved school massacres were bad enough but this latest killing is political dynamite, and if it goes off, my ass - and yours - will be going with it.'

CHAPTER 17

Lancaster was already sitting at a table when Yokely walked into the restaurant. He checked his watch – a chunky Rolex Submariner – but wasn't late. Lancaster nodded as Yokely sat down, but didn't speak until a waiter had poured coffee for Yokely and taken his breakfast order.

'The Senator has sent us the evidence from General Jackson's shooting,' said Lancaster as the waiter walked away. 'He says the Police Department and the FBI have come up with nothing that you couldn't get off the back of a cornflake packet and he's hoping we can give him a breakthrough.'

'I wish it was as easy as that,' said Yokely. 'Did you have any thoughts?'

Lancaster took a printed sheet from his jacket pocket. 'I've had a look at the ballistics report,' he said. 'Everyone was killed or wounded by small arms fire, except General Jackson, who was hit by a high calibre bullet, a 7.62 x 51 - that's a NATO standard round - from a sniper rifle. The angle of the wound - entry through the eye socket and exit wound at the base of the skull - consistent with him being hit by a shot fired from an upper floor apartment or a roof.' He paused. 'But something doesn't add up. The weapon must have been totally suppressed or firing a subsonic round.'

'Why do you say that?'

'Because no one heard the shot.'

'It could have been fired long distance. Half a mile away, maybe further if the shooter was a trained sniper.'

'But there were no buildings far away that offered an uninterrupted sightline,' said Lancaster. 'The only place that the shooter could have been was in a row of tenements about three hundred yards away. And our guys have already found the room where they think the sniper was holed up.'

'For sure?'

'Well they didn't find the gun or even spent casings, but there's no doubt. So like I said, it must have been a subsonic round or someone would have heard the shot. The shot had to have been fired from the tenements, but I don't know of any weapon that can effectively deliver a subsonic round over that distance.'

'I might be able to help you with that,' said Yokely. 'It's a sniper rifle the Special Forces use on hostage rescue operations. I've actually seen one in use, an Accuracy International PM. It's made by a British company. I'm pretty sure Delta Forces uses them on specialist missions. Let's go and have a look at the shooting scene.'

CHAPTER 18

Lancaster and Yokely drove to the square where General Jackson had been shot. The bloodstains had been scrubbed from the church steps, but a mound of flowers still marked the place where he had died.

'The sniper was on the top floor of the tenement building on the left,' Lancaster said, pointing to the far side of the square. 'If it was anything less than a subsonic round, people in the crowd would have heard the shot. Do you want a look-see?'

'Hell, yeah,' said Yokely

The two men walked across the square and over to the tenements. A bored uniformed cop was on guard duty and he waved them through after Lancaster flashed his FBI credentials. 'Are the CSIs still up there?' asked Lancaster.

'Long gone,' said the cop. 'Any idea how long I have to stand here?'

'Sorry,' said Lancaster. He headed up the stairs and Yokely followed.

'Excuse me!' shouted a voice behind them. A middle-aged man, balding with a five o'clock shadow was standing at the door with the cop. 'You're detectives, right?'

'FBI,' said Lancaster, heading back down the stairs.

'When can I have my apartment back?'

'You are?'

'Jake Crossland. I own the apartment.'

'Have the police spoken to you already?'

'Sure. I was downtown for the best part of three hours.' He gestured at the uniformed cop. 'This guy won't let me in.'

'It's a crime scene at the moment,' said Lancaster.

'Can I at least have a look at what state it's in?' said Crossland.

'Can't do any harm,' Yokely said to Lancaster.

Lancaster nodded at the cop. 'We'll escort Mr Crossland up and back,' he said.

'Sure,' said the cop.

Crossland hurried inside as if he was afraid the cop might change his mind, and the three men went upstairs. There was crime scene tape across the door. The landlord took his keys out but the door was unlocked and Lancaster opened it.

'So you haven't been in since the shooting?' Yokely asked the landlord.

'They wouldn't even let me into the building,' he said. 'As soon as I said it was my apartment they took me away.'

Yokely examined the window and the ledge, then turned to survey the room. As he looked up, his eye was caught by a scrap of black paper, Scotch-taped to the ceiling.

'How long has that been there?' he asked the landlord.

The landlord shrugged. 'Cleaners, they're all the same. Lazy bitches.'

'Yeah?' Yokely said. 'And I just bet you pay them top dollar too.' He fetched a rickety wooden chair from beside the wardrobe, stood on it and reached up, carefully detaching the tape and the piece of black paper. He climbed down and looked at it, then handed it to Lancaster.

Lancaster examined it with a frown, then shrugged. 'I've no idea what it is.'

'You tear up strips of black paper and hang it from the ceiling,' said Yokely. 'It breaks up the outlines of the room like the disruptive pattern camouflage on soldiers' combat gear. You'd be invisible to anyone looking up at the room from outside. It's another special forces trick.' He looked at the landlord. 'You met the tenant?'

'Just an ordinary Joe,' said the landlord. 'He paid a month's rent cash in advance.'

'That's unusual?'

'We don't get many tenants staying for a month. And we get even less who pay cash, in advance.'

'Did he have any luggage?'

'Not much. Just a suitcase, the sort with the wheels on the bottom and the retractable handle. Oh, and he'd stayed here before. Two, maybe three months ago. Only for one night.'

'You're sure?'

'I'm sure.'

CHAPTER 19

It had been four years since Yokely had last entered the sprawling base at Fort Bragg, North Carolina. There was no perimeter fence and no main gate, just a vast, endless plain littered with military ordnance and punctuated by the compounds of the individual units based there. The steel fences around the compound, topped by razor wire coils, looked like those of any other one, except for one significant difference. Miles of sun-bleached olive drab canvas hung along the inside of the fence, completely obscuring the Delta base from the outside world. He had decided to go in alone because the FBI and Delta Force didn't always get along. He had flown to Fayetteville Regional Airport and picked up a rental car to drive the 14 miles to Fort Bragg.

'Richard Yokely,' he said, showing his ID to the armed guard on the gate of the compound. 'I'm expected.'

'Good to see you back here, Sir,' the guard said. 'You won't remember me, I was just starting out with

Delta when you were here on detachment, but I heard a lot about you from the other guys.'

Yokely pulled up outside the headquarters building and was taken down a long corridor to the office of the commanding officer, who greeted him with a smile that was both broad and insincere. 'Well good to see you, Richard,' said the CO. 'But I guess this isn't a social call.' He paused and leaned back in his chair, putting his hands behind his head. 'So, what brings you down here in such an all-fired hurry?'

'I think one of your guys may have gone rogue.'

The CO brought his chair forward again with a thud. 'Bullshit. Everyone's psychologically screened. You should know better than anyone, they're the most well-trained and well-disciplined troops in the world.' He gave Yokely a hard look. 'What's your evidence anyway?'

Yokely had expected the reaction. He kept his voice low and his tone neutral. 'You know the hit on General Jackson? It was a long planned job, set up months before it was carried out. And a single head shot from over 300 yards, with a subsonic round: only a Special Forces sniper could do that.'

The CO shook his head. 'No way have any of my guys gone rogue. Special forces' tactics have been taught to every bunch of Cuban exiles, Nicaraguan contras, Iraqi dissidents, and just about every other group of anti-Communist Asians, Africans, Arabs and Latin Americans that the CIA has supported since Vietnam. If what you say is true, then you'll either find that your man is among them or he is one of the gun-nuts in the gun-clubs or the militias.'

'The guy I'm looking for is familiar with some very specialised equipment,' said Yokely. 'Specifically, the Accuracy International PM, or something similar capable of firing subsonic rounds with a high degree of accuracy.'

'That doesn't mean he's Delta.'

'It suggests that he could be. So what I'd like is to have a look at the records of all members of SFOD Delta who have left the unit in the last ten years.'

The CO took a long, slow breath and then exhaled just as slowly. He grinned when he saw Yokely staring at him. 'My daughter had been teaching me relaxation techniques,' he said. 'Helping to bring my blood pressure down.'

'How's that working out?'

The CO chuckled. 'It was fine up until I was told that one of my men might now be a terrorist stroke serial killer. So you'll be wanting what, the DA 2-1 forms for every man who left Delta in the past ten years, plus the DD 214?' The DA 2-1 form was a soldier's military service record, the DD 214 was the discharge record.

'Exactly,' said Yokely.

'With a view to what?'

'Locating them, seeing what they're up to.'

'Playing Santa Claus, trying to work out who's naughty and who's nice?'

'Something like that?'

'You realise that there will be hundreds of names. Delta Force is generally about a thousand strong, with perhaps a ten per cent turnover each year.'

'At the moment it would seem to be my only way forward,' said Yokely.

'Sooner you than me,' said the CO.

'How long before I can have the information?'

'It shouldn't take long, it's all on computer,' said the CO. 'I'll have to find out how easy it will be to get you the forms, but the names will be simple enough.'

Yokely's cellphone rang. He checked the screen. It was Lancaster. 'I'm sorry, I really need to take this,' he said, and the CO waved away his apology.

Yokely stood up and went over to the window. After a quick conversion with the FBI agent he ended the call and turned to smile at the CO. 'You can hang fire on the data dump,' he said. 'I think I have a short cut.'

'How come?'

'He set up a hiding post in one of the schools he attacked and the FBI's forensic team have come up with a DNA sample. He was smart enough to wear gloves all the time he was holed up, but he left some bodily fluid. Sweat or mucus probably, because it was probably as hot as hell where he was. You keep DNA samples of all your troops, don't you?'

'We have done for years,' said the CO. The days of relying on dogtags for ID are long gone, now we keep DNA and fingerprints on file.'

Yokely held out his phone. 'If you use this Dropbox link, you'll get the full DNA profile.'

The CO spent ten minutes tapping on his computer keyboard, then he sat back and waved at a service record that was up on his screen. 'Earl Long,' he said. 'Former NCO. I don't remember him, unfortunately.'

Yokely pecred at the screen. There was a photograph of a tall, powerful black man in combat fatigues. Yokely zeroed in on the face, framed by the standard US forces' buzz cut hair. There was a small crinkled scar on one cheekbone and Long's eyes seemed almost to be leached of pigment. He appeared to stare through the camera, as if indifferent to how it recorded him.

He frowned as he studied Long's record. Long had expressed his disquiet about the conduct of the war in Afghanistan. It was one of a litany of complaints recorded in his file, and had led, no doubt, to the subsequent entry: 'Unsuitable for further promotion.'

The final entry on his record read 'Recommended for medical discharge.'

'Not much to go on there,' Yokely said. 'Mother and father deceased. Wife deceased. No siblings. His next of kin is his mother-in-law. That's unusual. How about someone who served with him? Someone who might be able to give me some background on Long?'

The CO spent another five minutes tapping on his keyboard, then he sat back. 'I've got a name for you, a guy who spent quite a bit of time with Long. Eric Keinstrom. They did two tours in Afghanistan and one in Iraq together.'

'Is he on the base?'

'No, he left soon after Long. But you won't have any trouble locating him. And I doubt he'll be too busy to talk to you.'

Yokely phoned Senator Adams as he drove back to the airport. 'We have an ID,' he said. 'Guy by the name of Earl Long. Former Delta.'

'Well done,' said the Senator. 'How soon before you can get to him?'

'There isn't a current address on file, but I'm going to talk to an Army buddy of his and his next of kin.'

'The clock is ticking, Richard. There's every chance that he will strike again and soon.'

'I'm aware of that, Senator. I'm on the case.'

'And this Long. What sort of man is he?'

'Very experienced. Demolition skills, qualified sniper, he's a regular killing machine.'

'Ethnic background?'

'He's black if that's what you're asking, Senator.'

The Senator swore under his breath. 'That's all we need,' he said. 'A black man killing white kids.'

'The victims weren't just white, Senator. There were blacks, Hispanics. Asians. Long appears to be an equal opportunities killer.'

'Agreed, but the majority of the victims are white and that's what the Press will go for. We can't have that happening, Richard. This needs to be dealt with in Grey Fox style. If it gets out that there's a racist angle to the killings, there'll be a backlash that will hurt everyone.'

'I hear you, Senator.'

'Good man. I know I can trust you on this.'

The Senator ended the call and Yokely gritted his teeth as he drove. He had no reservations about killing people. That was his job. And the people he killed usually had what was coming to them. But Earl Long was an American hero, a warrior who had served his country and served it well. Admittedly he was now a rogue warrior, but something had put Long on the path he was on and whatever it was deserved to be investigated. There couldn't be any excuse for the atrocities that Long had committed, but there might well be a reason. Clearly the Senator wasn't interested in any motivation that Long might have had, he just wanted him dead.

CHAPTER 20

Early the next morning Yokely and Lancaster flew up to New York City and by lunchtime they were standing before a huge steel door. As they waited for it to open they scrutinised the warning sign next to it. 'Rikers Island Penitentiary. The following items are prohibited ...'

The gate slid open, revealing an inner steel mesh barrier. Beyond it a razor wire fence enclosed an exercise yard crowded with shuffling figures. Lancaster showed his FBI ID and they were led into an interview room. A few minutes later a powerful square-jawed figure was ushered in to sit on the other side of the Plexiglas screen. He stared at Lancaster for several seconds, then nodded. 'You're a Fed.' He turned his gaze on Yokely, then shrugged. 'You I can't place.'

'The name's Richard,' said Yokely. 'You're Eric Keinstrom?'

'If I'm not then you've really wasted your time, haven't you?' He forced a smile. 'Yeah. I'm Keinstrom. They call me Sparky. What do you want?'

'What are you in for?'

Sparky gestured at the FBI agent. 'I'm sure you read the rap sheet before you got here. I hung around for a while, but couldn't find a job that was worth a bucket of spit, so I got to thinking, why not put all that training at breaking into places to some purpose.' He grinned. 'I was pretty good at it too.'

'Not that good or we wouldn't be having this conversation here,' said Yokely.

'That wasn't down to me. My lady friend and I had a little difference of opinion. She thought I was two-timing her - rightly as it happens. She got mad and turned me in. She gave them chapter and verse and told them where to find every last cent … except the stash she took off with, of course.' He eyed Yokely narrowly through the screen. 'But you didn't come here to ask me about that, did you?'

'No I didn't,' Yokely said. 'I came to ask you about Earl Long.'

Sparky looked suddenly serious. 'Is he okay?'

'Why do you ask?'

'He's not dead, is he?'

Yokely's eyes narrowed. 'Why would you think that?'

'Last time I saw him he was …. let's say depressed.'

'PTSD?'

'I'm not a doctor or a shrink. Let's just say he wasn't a happy bunny and leave it at that.'

'What was he like? As a soldier?'

Sparky leaned back in his chair. 'Shorty? He was quite a character. A bit of a loner and a nonconformist.

He was a damn good soldier and a brilliant planner, best I ever worked with. He did a lot of black operations, and I'd say he was part of most of the good ops that we did: Iraq, some in Afghanistan, a hit in the Bekaa Valley, all that kind of stuff. He was one hell of a sniper too. He had a mind like a computer. He could factor in the range, the wind - shit, he'd even calculate the humidity - and then put his first shot into the target every time. He had more patience than anyone I knew as well; he didn't care if he had to stay in a hide for a month, as long as he got his shot at the end of it. And I've watched him cross open ground without a shred of cover, belly crawling like a snake, changing camouflage four, five, even six times, and if I hadn't known he was there, I'd never have seen him.'

'You called him Shorty?'

'Everyone did. Because of his name and because he was tall. You know how nicknames work.'

'I never had a nickname,' said Yokely.

'Not even Tricky Dicky?'

Yokely flashed him a tight smile. 'Most definitely not that,' he said. 'What about yours? Sparky? Demolition?'

Sparky grinned. 'My name. It means "no electricity" in German.' He shrugged. 'You don't get to choose your nickname.'

'What about Shorty's weaknesses, his character flaws?' Yokely asked.

'Well, he seemed to carry some baggage around with him, something that had gone down in his past

I guess, and he could be a regular barrack-room lawyer at times, always moaning about the way the Pentagon was treating us. Nothing unusual in that of course, most of us did, and I guess he had more reason than most.'

'What do you mean?'

'When Shorty came back from Iraq, he married his childhood sweetheart, Kimberley. They grew up together in a tough part of Baltimore. The way Shorty told it, they got engaged when they were six. Anyway, they moved into a small house on the outskirts of Fayetteville, so as to be close to Delta HQ. They used the rest of his leave for a honeymoon in Vegas. As soon as he returned to duty, Shorty was sent to Afghanistan. We were there together. He got a letter there from Kim; she was carrying his son. They had a daughter too, but Shorty was just desperate for a son that he could take fishing and play football with - you've never seen a man so happy when he got the news. He wrote to Kim every day while he was there, but that had to end a few weeks later, when we were infiltrated into the bandit country on the Afghan-Pakistan border.'

He leaned forward and Yokely could see the man was tensing up. 'The job was the usual stuff - intelligence gathering, ambush, assassination, sabotage, terror - in preparation for a major advance into Taliban territory. Anyway, within a short time, Shorty began to feel ill. He had pains in his limbs that he said seemed to start inside his bones, he was always short of breath, and he lost weight and strength. He tried to ignore it and carry on, but eventually he had to be pulled out. He was flown to Dhahran and examined by the army doctors. After weeks of tests that left him even sicker, he was evacuated back to the States. He never spoke about it to me, but I heard that Kim had also gotten real sick while he was away. She died before he got home.'

'And the baby?'

'Never drew a breath. It died when she did. Anyways, like I said, he never spoke about it and I never asked. I figured if he wanted to talk, he would, and if he didn't, that was his privilege.'

He paused and held Yokely's gaze. 'Shorty went a little weird after that, though God knows, he had reason to. By the time I next saw him he was back on operational service. The army medics never found anything wrong with him, but he got real paranoid about his illness. He blamed the depleted uranium munitions we'd been using. Nobody really knew for sure what was wrong, but a few of the guys thought it was just bullshit - some fake disease to hide the fact that he'd lost his nerve. Shorty got in a couple of fights with guys who were sick of his bellyaching.'

'Was he discharged for that?'

'Not until a while later. He argued with the Troop Officer at the briefing before an op, said it was a sui-cide mission. He was pulled straight off the op and left behind when the other guys from his Troop went in.' He gave a bleak smile. 'Maybe he wasn't so weird after all. He was right about the op anyway. When it all went to rat-shit, the rest of us - even Shorty - had to go in as the Immediate Action to support the others until we could withdraw. We were airborne on the copters on our way in, when the word came through to turn back. The guys already on the ground were left to fend for themselves.' He shook his head at the memory. 'We lost some good men that day.'

'Where did the order to pull out come from?'

'The top.'

'The very top?'

'It don't get any higher. Dead Americans on TV make for bad news for politicians. Half a dozen is bad enough, but four or five times that number and it's so long to a second term.'

'And Shorty?'

'When we got back to base, he shot dead the Afghan translator he suspected of betraying the op to the Taliban. The Troop Officer wanted him court-martialled and dishonourably discharged but he was given a medical discharge instead - a face-saver all round. Hell of a shame though, like I said, he was a damn good soldier.'

There was a long silence. 'So what happened to him?' Yokely said. 'Have you seen him since?'

Sparky shook his head. 'Not since the day he left Delta.' He gestured around him. 'And he sure as hell isn't in here.'

'Any ideas where he might be? We need to find him.'

'What's the problem? Is Shorty in trouble?'

Yokely nodded. 'I'm afraid so.'

'Big trouble?'

'The biggest.'

'But you can't tell me?'

'I'm sorry. But trust me, Eric, he'll be a lot safer if I'm the one who finds it.'

'You're former Delta?'

'My CV's classified, Eric. Let's leave it at that. So where would he go, assuming he couldn't go back to the family house?'

'He always said he felt safest in Baltimore. He was from a place called Winchester, though the locals called it Sandtown. He never stopped talking about the place. He told me that the name Sandtown comes from the trails of sand the old horse-drawn wagons used to spill on the unpaved streets as they rumbled back into Baltimore from the old sand and gravel quarries. Some parts are okay, but most of it is pretty rugged. From what Shorty said, you definitely wouldn't want to be taking a stroll there after dark. Violent crime rates are about 150 per 1000 people there, so the chance of being a victim is worse than one in seven. According to the DEA, one in ten of the population of Baltimore as a whole is addicted to heroin, so you can guess how high the percentage is round Sandtown. Oh, and the murder rate is four-teen times New York City's.'

'And that's where he felt safe?' said Lancaster, who had making notes in a small notepad.

'He was born there. His parents died when he was quite young and he stayed with some distant relatives and I think the man of the house was a bit free with his hands. Shorty spent most of his childhood on the streets.' He forced a smile. 'He had a shit childhood but it was probably what made him such a great soldier.'

'That tends to be the way it works,' said Yokely.

'Yeah, tell me about it,' said Sparky. He sat back and folded his muscular arms. 'Are we done?'

Yokely nodded. 'Yeah, we're done.'

CHAPTER 21

Yokely picked up a rental car not far from the prison and drove to Baltimore. It was a three and a half hour drive to the trailer park where Shorty's mother-in-law lived, and Yokely did all the driving, Lancaster spent most of his time scrolling through information on his smart phone.

Freda Wyatt was sitting on a kitchen chair next to the door of her trailer, drinking a soda when Yokely pulled up. They climbed out of the car and curtains started twitching in several of the trailers. Yokely figured that men in suits rarely turned up with good news. Through the open door they could see three children lying on the floor watching cartoons on the TV. Mrs Wyatt was running to fat, and the corners of her mouth were permanently down-turned as if in reaction to the hand life had dealt her. She was wearing a shapeless dress spotted with stains on the front and on her head was a badly-fitting wig which had tilted to one side.

She heard Yokely out in silence as he explained why they were there. Yokely didn't mention the fact that they thought her son-in-law was a suspected terrorist or serial killer, and instead sold her on the idea that they represented the Army's welfare department. 'We're anxious to trace Earl so that he can get what he's owed,' he said. 'Have you seen him recently?'

'I haven't seen him in over a year,' she said. 'And he never was much of a one for keeping in touch. Not that we were what you'd call close. He and my husband - ' She shook her head. 'My ex-husband that is, never did see eye to eye. But what happened to my daughter brought us together a little. He came here every year on the anniversary of her death to put flowers on her grave. But this year he never showed up.'

'I know this will be hard for you,' Yokely said, 'but if you could tell us a little bit more about your daughter's death it would be very helpful.' He reached forward and touched the other woman's arm. 'I'm sorry to ask you this, I know it must be very painful to call up the memories.'

Freda nodded. 'I thought it would get easier with the years. It never has. There isn't a day goes past, that I don't think about her still.'

After the silence had built for a minute Yokely gave her a gentle prompt. 'Were you there when Earl came back from abroad?'

She nodded. 'I was at the hospital with her. It was so sudden, we hadn't been able to let him know. He was frantic with worry; he kept trying to call home but all he got was the ringing tone echoing down the line. Among the bundle of mail waiting for him at

Fort Bragg was an envelope containing a photograph of Kim's sonogram. Along the edge she had written three words: "That's our boy!" He was still clutching it in his hand when he showed up at the hospital.'

As Yokely listened to her he could almost see Long standing there, tears scalding his eyes as he stared and stared at the tiny, dimly outlined figure of his child.

'The next letter he opened was the note I'd left, telling him that Kim had been taken to the Military Hospital.' She paused, fumbling in her purse for a tissue. She dabbed at her eyes, then twisted it between her fingers as she spoke. 'Kim had gotten some abnormalities, I think they called them, in her pregnancy that had led to leukemia. The doctors were doing what they could, battling to save her and the baby, but they warned us to be ready for the worst. It was almost too much for Earl to take. Kim was deeply unconscious, her breathing so shallow and faint you could hardly hear it, but he sat down, held her hand and began talking to her as if she could understand every word. Eventually her eyelids flickered. Her eyes opened and focussed on him. 'Honey, you're back,' she said, her voice so low he had to stoop to hear it. Then her eyes closed and she gave a breath like a long, slow sigh. A moment later the alarms started to shriek. She died and the baby died with her.'

When Freda had recovered her poise, Yokely asked her what had happened to Earl after that. 'There was still Louella,' she said, 'my granddaughter. She was so much like her mother - two peas in a pod. Earl tried to care for her, but every time he looked at her, all he could see was Kim and hard though he tried, I guess he kinda blamed her for not being her mother. They came back to Baltimore. He said he felt safe here.'

'Where did they live?' asked Lancaster.

'Sandtown,' she said. 'Earl sold their place in North Carolina and he rented a row house.'

'Do you have the address?'

She shook her head. 'He doesn't live there any more. Not after what happened.'

Yokely took a step towards her. 'What did happen?' he asked.

She took a deep breath before continuing. 'They used to row a lot and with no mom to look after her, she became a pretty wild child, missing school, mixing in some bad company and often getting into trouble. She'd pretty much moved out by the time she was sixteen and anyway, when Earl found work as a carpenter with a company that did big contracts for hotels and corporations and such, he was often away travelling the country and she was left to her own devices.'

Tears started to her eyes again and she dabbed at them with a tissue. 'It was while he was away on one of those trips that Louella was killed. It was just the most terrible irony. She hadn't been in high school in weeks, but she was threatened with being taken into care or sent to juve if she didn't go, so she started turning up again. The second day she was there, a kid who'd been excluded from the school and had a history of mental illness, showed up armed with an assault rifle he'd bought at a gun show. He killed seven kids and wounded plenty more; Louella was one of the victims.' Her mouth twisted into a grimace. 'I'm guessing you won't have read or heard much about it, because Louella and all the other victims were black or mixed race and, unlike shootings in white high schools, them kind of killings don't rate much on the national news.'

'This was here, in Baltimore?'

She nodded. 'I think it tipped Earl right over the edge. He kept bombarding the news channels with complaints and making threats against everyone he saw as responsible for Louella's death - not so much the shooter, as the school, the authorities, the politicians and the gun rights lobby, that had made it possible. He lost his job because of it and I ain't seen hide nor hair of him since, but I did hear he was living on the streets.'

'He had money, though? From his work and the sale of his house.'

'I wouldn't know about that,' she said. 'I just heard he was homeless and not looking in a good state.'

CHAPTER 22

Yokely and Lancaster booked into the Marriott Hotel, close to Baltimore's Inner Harbour tourist centre. They had adjoining rooms and after they had both freshened up, Yokely joined the FBI agent in his room.

'I researched the shooting,' said Lancaster. 'She was right. Seven kids dead and one of them was Long's daughter.'

'So the death of his daughter was some sort of trigger,' said Yokely. 'He goes through all sorts of shit out in the Sandbox, loses his wife and unborn son and then a school shooter takes out the last child.'

'And he reacts by killing innocent children? Shooting the general, I can understand. Going after politicians, the NRA, that would make sense. But this guy broke into schools and killed children.'

'We don't know what his PTSD levels were,' said Yokely. 'He could have been a time bomb ready to go off and losing his daughter pushed him over the edge.'

'He'd have to be insane to start killing children.'

'I'm not arguing with you,' said Yokely. 'There's clearly a mental problem. But in his twisted mind, perhaps there's a logic to it. His child died in a school shooting, so he wants them to feel the pain he felt. The exact same pain.'

Lancaster shook his head. 'I could never kill a child,' he said.

'You can't say that,' said Yokely. 'You haven't gone through what he went through. It tipped him over the edge. It could happen to anyone.'

'And he killed the general because he was unhappy at what happened to him in the army?'

'Perhaps, yes. Again, there is a logic to it.'

'And the arson attack?'

'He's lashing out, using the skills he acquired with Delta.'

The FBI agent sighed and shook his head. 'I can't get my head around it.'

'His fingerprint was in the crawlspace. He has the skills. He was a sniper. And he's gone missing. It's him, Neil.'

'I get that. I just don't understand why he's doing it.'

'Because you're not in his mindset. Long is crazy, if you accept that then you just have to accept that what he's doing is a result of his mental illness. It doesn't make sense to you but in his screwed-up mind it probably makes perfect sense.' He went over to the minibar and helped himself to two miniature whiskies that he poured into a glass, then sat down on one of the two beds in the room. 'The question isn't why he's doing what he's doing, it's how are we going to stop him.'

'We have to find him first. Obviously,' said the FBI agent, sitting down on the other bed. 'Do you think he has returned to Sandtown?'

'His mother-in-law seemed to think so. So did Keinstrom. And it makes sense. He's comfortable there, it's familiar territory. He'll feel safe. If he was fully sane he'd realise that it would be the obvious place to look for him, but that ship has clearly sailed. How easy would it be to find him in Sandtown?'

Lancaster shrugged. 'The district covers the area east of US Highway 1, north of West Lafayette and west of North Fremont Avenue, which becomes Pennsylvania Avenue. Baltimore Police has its Western Division HQ there and believe me that isn't a coincidence. If you're African-American and looking for a place to disappear off the radar, Sandtown is just about perfect. By every statistical index, it's one of the poorest and most crime-ridden and drug-addled districts in the entire US of A. So people there mind their business and they sure as hell don't talk to cops.'

'Have you been there?'

'I've passed through it. But I've checked it out on Google Maps, I can show you around.'

Fifteen minutes later they were in Yokely's rental car, driving around West Baltimore. It was one of the most deprived areas of the city and the Sandtown district was the most decrepit part of it. Most of the houses were in terraces and built of brick or stone, though most had subsequently been re-faced with synthetic stone cladding in a variety of styles. From time to time, attempts had been made to gentrify some streets, but the developers seemed to be fighting a losing battle against the tide of poverty and crime, signalled by wastelands and empty lots, boarded up and derelict houses, burned out cars, used condoms, syringes and crack-pipes. The only businesses still standing were mainly liquor stores protected by heavy gauge steel mesh and shutters, and even they were so dilapidated that it was hard to know if they were still trading.

'It's like Helmand on a bad day,' said Yokely as they drove slowly through Sandtown, attracting suspicious or hostile looks from the few people they saw on the streets.

'But with added crack and crystal meth,' Lancaster said. 'But you're not wrong, it is a war zone. Baltimore tries to promote itself as "Charm City" but if you've ever seen The Wire, you'll have seen its alternative nickname: "Bodymore Murdaland".' He grinned. 'Sounds better if you say it in a Baltimore accent.'

'I guess Long will still be known around here,' said Yokely. 'We need to get out and start asking around.'

Lancaster shook his head. 'No one here is going to talk to you,' he said.

'Because I'm the wrong colour?'

'That, and the fact that you're wearing a real estate agent's blazer and have tassels on your shoes,' said the FBI agent. 'I'm the right colour but they won't talk to me because they'll know straight away that I'm a Fed.'

'So what do we do?'

'If it was my call, I'd get the Baltimore PD to sweep through the place. The last thing the people around here want is a police presence, with any luck someone will give up Long just to get some peace and quiet.'

'The boys in blue are bad for business?'

'Exactly,' said Lancaster.

'I'll see what I can arrange,' said Yokely.

'You can do that?'

Yokely grinned. 'Let's just say I have friends in high places.'

'Can I ask you a question?'

'Sure, you can ask. I can't promise an answer.'

'When they said I was to ride shotgun with you, they didn't tell me who you were with, just that the White House was sending you.'

'That's true enough.'

'So you work for the President?'

'Indirectly.'

'And you're on the case because you have a special forces background?'

'I won't deny that, but like I told Kleinstrom in Rikers, my CV is classified.'

'Fair enough. And you helped us identify Long. Our guys hadn't found the hide in the school and probably never would have. And you got Delta Force to fast track the DNA matching.'

'As I said, friends in high places.'

'And I get that. But we know who he is now. Why don't you just hand this over to the FBI and the cops? Get his picture and details out there and bring him in.'

'Because this guy is a professional. Traditional dragnets won't work. He's used to evading capture in hostile environments. And if he knows we're on to him, he'll be even harder to find.'

Lancaster folded his arms and stared through the windshield.

'Are you okay?' asked Yokely.

'Are we trying to capture him, or are you on the case for a different reason?' Lancaster asked eventually.

'Why do you say that?'

'Because I get the feeling that you've got a lot in common with this Earl Long. And it might save everyone a lot of trouble if the problem was to just …. disappear.'

Yokely smiled. 'And you think that's what I do? I make problems disappear?'

Lancaster nodded. 'Yeah. Am I wrong?'

'Neil, my friend, I'm afraid we're now in the realms of questions I can't answer.'

'Because if you do, you'll have to kill me?'

Yokely laughed and patted the man's leg. 'Whoever said the FBI have no sense of humour?' he said.

Chapter 23

Yokely waited until he was alone in his room at the Marriott before phoning Senator Adams and explaining what he wanted. 'A house to house? In Sandtown?' the Senator said. 'Are you crazy? That area is practically a no-go area for the cops.'

'There's every chance that Long is using the area as his base,' said Yokely. 'His mother-in-law thought he was homeless but I'm sure he's got money. The equipment he has been using doesn't come cheap. But it makes sense for him to be dressing like he's on the street.'

'The Chief Of Police won't be happy,' said the Senator.

'I'm sure you can sell it to him,' said Yokely.

'But we can't let it be known what we want him for. That'd go public within minutes and that's the last thing we want.'

'I'm sure you'll come up with a decent cover story,' said Yokely. 'How about you say he's picked up a communicable disease while he was out in Afghanistan? Get a flyer printed out from the Centre For Disease Control.'

'If the media got hold of that, they'd go crazy. We need a search carried out, but with no publicity,' said the Senator.

'Something simple, then. Wanted in questioning for a cop shooting in another state, maybe.'

'That might work,' said the Senator. 'Where are you?'

'In Baltimore,' said Yokely.

'Stay put and I'll get the ball rolling,' said the Senator.

Yokely had a quick shower, then went outside to smoke one of his small cigars. He was surprised to see Lancaster there, smoking a cigarette. 'I didn't have you down as a smoker,' said Yokely, as he lit up a cigar.

'I tend not to broadcast the fact,' said Lancaster. 'These days cigarettes and alcohol can be promotion killers. Being overweight is a no-no. And God help you if you say the wrong thing on social media.'

'I've never been a fan of Facebook or Twitter,' said Yokely. He blew smoke up at the darkening sky. 'And certainly never been a fan of expressing opinions in public.'

'I shut down my Facebook page but then I was told that's a red flag, too,' said Lancaster. 'You need to have a public page so they can check that you've got the right mindset. It's a minefield.'

'But you're doing all right?'

Lancaster nodded. 'I know how to play the game,' he said. 'But if it gets worse, I might look for another career.' He took a long pull on his cigarette, held it deep in his lungs, then exhaled slowly. 'I'm sorry if I came on a bit strong in the car.'

'No problem,' said Yokely. 'You have a right to know what's going on.'

'I wasn't being judgmental,' said the FBI agent. 'Earl Long needs to be stopped. No question of that.'

'It's a complicated situation,' said Yokely.

'Because he's black?'

Yokely looked at him as he drew on his cigar and blew more smoke at the sky. 'I think the powers that be are worried about copycats,' he said. 'And perhaps a backlash against the black community. If word got out that a black killer was targeting white kids ....' He shrugged. 'It doesn't take much to get racists fired up these days.'

'Except that he's not targeting white kids. There have been black victims. And Asians.'

'Facts don't always get reported,' said Yokely. 'Most newspapers and TV channels have their own agenda these days. All the public will see is a black killer and white victims.' He shrugged. 'Anyway, the plan is that it won't be made public.' He looked at his watch. 'I'm going to grab a club sandwich and a coffee in the bar. Probably follow it up with a few malt whiskies. Are you up for it?'

Lancaster laughed and flicked ash into the road. 'So long as you promise not to tell my bosses.'

'Your secrets are safe with me,' said Yokely.

Lancaster nodded. 'Yeah, I'm sure they are,' he said.

CHAPTER 24

Yokely was woken by his phone's ringtone early the next morning, and groped for it, still rubbing the sleep from his eyes. He recognised Senator Adams's voice at once. 'Sorry to wake you, Richard, but it's been a short night for all of us. There's been an explosion in Sandtown in Baltimore. They think it was a bomb.'

'Text the location and I'll be there as fast as possible,' Yokely said. He jumped out of bed, grabbed a robe and hurried down the corridor to Lancaster's room. He knocked on the door and when the sleepy FBI agent answered, told him to get dressed and meet him downstairs. Yokely himself was dressed and at the wheel of his rental car in less than ten minutes and Lancaster hurried out just two minutes later. Yokely handed Lancaster his phone with the address and the FBI agent called out directions as they threaded their way through West Baltimore to the site of the explosion. They parked behind a logjam of police, fire department and bomb squad vehicles, a safe distance from the building where the explosion had occurred.

Yokely glanced at the run-down buildings and weed-strewn waste lots that surrounded them. The building, a nondescript four-storey warehouse, looked little different from its neighbours. The only clue to what had happened was a gaping, blackened window-frame on the ground-floor and a smudged, smoky outline, like a flame drawn in charcoal, leading from it up the outside of the building.

A small crowd of curious onlookers had gathered at the cordon of yellow crime scene tape thrown up around the area, and an ever-growing media army had commandeered one of the waste lots with a view of the building. Two TV reporters were already delivering speculative pieces to camera as Lancaster showed his FBI ID to a couple of bored-looking uniformed cops manning the cordon. Yokely and the FBI agent ducked under the tapes and headed for the building.

The sun-blistered paint on the gable showed it had once been a food importer's warehouse, but from the newer-looking signs clustered around the doorway, Yokely judged it was now home to at least a dozen small businesses. A group of figures clad in blue forensic suits were standing around the back of a bomb squad vehicle, smoking cigarettes and drinking cups of coffee brought from a Burger King in a less run-down district a few blocks north. It was easy to identify the lead detective, a tall, black-haired man in his late forties, because the others were deferring to him as they discussed what they had found.

Lancaster walked over and held out his hand, show-ing his ID in the other one. 'Neil Lancaster,' he said, 'hope you don't mind if my colleague and I join you on this.'

The detective ignored his outstretched hand and gave him a suspicious look. 'You got here quickly.' He nodded at Yokely. 'Mike Donovan. I'm in charge at the moment but I think that'll change soon.'

'What's the story, Mike?' asked Yokely.

'There was a shooting near here yesterday - not exactly unusual in West Baltimore, but still. The local police were in the area as part of the house to house enquiries we'd been asked to carry out. The perp was seen running towards the warehouse. When they searched the building, the perp was nowhere to be seen - but he was probably just a punk kid anyway, not the man we were looking for - but the tenant for one of the ground floor workshops was nowhere to be found and the owner's keys didn't fit any more because the locks had been changed and the door had been reinforced with steel. The officers became suspicious and after a sniffer dog gave sign that it had smelled explosives, they obtained a search war-rant and broke down the door. The first man into the room must have triggered a bomb. The dog was killed and the officer badly wounded, though the paramedics reckon he's got a chance of pulling through. That's as much as I know. I just happened to be first in line in the incident room when the call came in.'

'So what about the blast?' asked Yokely. 'Was it definitely caused by explosives?'

Donovan spread his hands. 'We'll have to wait for the forensics reports of course, but I tell you what, this wasn't no gas explosion.'

'Is the scene clear?' asked Yokely.

The detective nodded. 'We're just finishing up. No other bombs.'

'Mind if we take a look around?'

'Be my guest.' Donovan reached into the back of the truck and handed over two pairs of white overalls, blue shoe covers and latex gloves. Yokely and Lancaster put them on and then followed the detective into the building.

The lobby was bathed in the harsh glare of arc lights rigged by the bomb squad. Yokely sniffed the air. It smelled of smoke and damp, and the stale stench of human piss, but in among it he could also detect the acrid odour of explosives.

The heavy, steel-lined door to his right stood open, hanging from one hinge, and beyond it he could see a blue-clad crime scene investigator moving among the debris. He ran his fingers over the surface of the door and gave each of the locks a minute examination, then straightened up and stepped into the room. Donovan followed him in, but stood back a couple of paces as Yokely and Lancaster looked around.

The bomb had blown a crater in the concrete floor just inside the door. The twisted and severed ends of a water pipe protruded from the sides of the hole. The Fire Department had cut off the supply but a trickle of water still dribbled from the broken pipe.

Yokely edged his way round the crater into the room. The single window opening was high up in the wall; the workshop could as easily have been a basement, a lock-up or a grubby apartment.

The outer walls were blackened by smoke and there was a gaping hole where part of the ceiling had collapsed. Fallen plaster and debris from the wrecked shelves hanging off the walls lay inches deep on the floor. There were puddles of water among it.

Donovan shook his head. 'Those Fire Department boys certainly know how to fuck up the evidence, don't they?'

Yokely nodded. 'But if they didn't put the fire out, the only evidence you'd have would be ashes.' He stood motionless, his gaze raking the devastated room, taking in every detail. The workbench had been blown across the room by the blast. Yokely stood next to it, his eyes shut, trying to picture the scene, imagining the bomb maker at work in the cramped room. He shivered and opened his eyes. A vice was fixed to the far end of the bench and a few tiny shreds of a bright, silvery metal were still visible in the cracks in its surface. Yokely began to move slowly around the room, turning over the debris, picking up and scrutinising item after item from among the rubble on the floor.

He found bits of a soldering iron, pieces of wire, fragments of circuit boards and shards of plastic casings. There were micro-switches and timing devices, including one cannibalised from a DVD recorder, and programmable to the minute up to 365 days ahead, packs of batteries, bottles of detergents and chemicals, and a drum of sodium chlorate. The plastic container was blackened and slightly melted.

Yokely turned it over in his hands. 'If the Fire Department had gotten here about a minute later, this would have gone up as well.'

'What do you reckon this is from?' Donovan said, holding up a broken piece of curved glass, the size of a small bowl.

'It looks like an oscilloscope,' said Yokely. 'The perp must have been thinking about making a radio-controlled device. I'm pretty sure the oscilloscope would have told him there are just too many ambient radio waves in urban areas these days and a stray radio signal could have detonated the bomb prematurely. He could have used one of those micro-switches instead, but he'd know that every single manufactured item carries a code or identifying number. The IRA once used a mechanical timer from a heating boiler to detonate a bomb in London. From the microscopic fragments they recovered in a fingertip search, the police were able to trace it back to the shop that had originally supplied it. The IRA bombing campaign forced the British police to become the world leaders in this area of forensics, but everything they knew, they shared with the USA. If the Brits know how to do it, the FBI certainly does too. The man we're looking for would have known that too; that's why he went for a low-tech timer instead.'

He stooped down again and teased some scraps of burned paper from among the debris. He stared at them, frowning in concentration. He picked up a few of the scraps and squinted at them. One of them was from a brochure and there were NRA contact details on it. Donovan looked over his shoulder. 'What's that?'

'Something to do with the NRA,' said Yokely. 'See if you can find more pieces.'

'You think our guy is a gun nut?

'The jury's still out on that,' said Yokely.

Donovan and Lancaster helped look for more scraps of burned paper but nothing they found seemed to match up with what Yokely had found.

Yokely moved back to the bomb crater and began searching around the edge, clearing away the debris with his fingertips until he found what he was seeking: the charred end of a piece of electrical flex. He eased it clear of the rubble, and gently pulled on it, exposing a few more inches of the wire. He followed it along the foot of the inside wall to the far corner of the room.

There it began to climb the wall towards the infra red motion detector. It was smoke-blackened but otherwise undamaged. Yokely carefully wiped away the soot and then examined the casing. There was a network of tiny scratches around the hole in its base. He took off the cover and exposed the safety switch.

'Here's the trigger,' he said. Donovan and Lancaster joined him. 'When the motion sensor picked up the movement of someone opening the door, the bomb was set to detonate in a few seconds unless the circuit was interrupted by pushing some sort of non-metallic pin - something like a match or a golf tee - into the hole on the base.'

Donovan gave a low whistle. 'That cop is lucky to be alive.'

Yokely nodded, still staring at the device. 'But the primary aim of the booby-trap wasn't necessarily to kill intruders.' He pointed to the hole in the wall where the window had been blown out. 'That's what all this was for.'

Donovan and Lancaster exchanged blank looks. 'I don't get you,' Donovan said.

Yokely spoke in a monotone, his back still turned to them as he stared at the device. 'Special Forces do this as routine; you booby-trap any site like a hide or a lying up place that you're planning to return to. When you approach it, you first circle around it at a distance to make sure that it's intact. If the booby-trap's been detonated, you just keep right on going. If it's killed a few of the enemy as well, fine; but the primary aim is not to act as a weapon against the intruder but as a warning to the person who set the booby-trap.'

'So this is Long's base?'

'It was, for sure,' said Yokely.

Donovan was staring at him. 'You know who it is, don't you?'

'Probably, and I certainly know what he is. We're facing a guy who's fighting a war, and it's not for the first time.' He paused. 'And if we don't catch him, he can make everyone's worst nightmare come true.' He wiped the sweat from his brow. 'I've seen enough. Let's go.'

As Yokely and Lancaster walked back down the street to the car, Yokely turned to look back at the burned, empty window frame of the workshop. 'He'll know we're on his trail now,' he said. 'And he'll be pretty sure we know who he is as well.'

CHAPTER 25

Shorty did not even need to return to his former base to know that it had been compromised, for the explosion and the injury to the cop were all over the evening news, though the headlines were mainly about the sniffer dog that had been killed. A Maryland congressman was interviewed and he called for a posthumous medal to be awarded, not to the policeman who in any case was recovering, but to the dog.

Shorty did not go back to Baltimore again; even to be seen anywhere in the city or the surrounding area might put him at risk and he could not afford to let his guard down now, so close to his goal. Instead he drove west to St Louis, Missouri, within striking distance of his target, but far enough away to avoid the risk of compromise. It was a thirteen-hour drive but he did it in one stretch, drinking half a dozen cups of black coffee on the way.

He found a place in St Louis, paid the owner cash rent, a month in advance and after a lengthy series of counter-surveillance manoeuvres, it was almost dark when he returned to his new base and unlocked the door. It was another anonymous room, a damp basement, with paint peeling from the walls. A bare light bulb hung from the ceiling and a pair of cheap plastic curtains obscured the window. There was the constant noise of heavy traffic, making the window rattle in its frame, and every minute, as regular as a clock, there was the roar of a jet passing overhead.

CHAPTER 26

The next day, forensics experts at the FBI were able to identify the fragment of paper that Yokely had found in the burned house in Sandtown. It came from an NRA brochure that was being used to promote the forthcoming NRA annual meeting at the Kansas City convention centre.

Lancaster brought the news to Yokely in the bar of the Marriott Hotel where he was on his second whisky. According to Lancaster, there had also been burnt fragments from a large-scale map of the Kansas City area. 'So that's his target?' said the FBI agent. 'He's going after the NRA? That's what all this is about?'

'It looks that way,' said Yokely. 'He seems to be lashing out at anyone he thinks is responsible for his situation.'

'But a soldier taking his anger out on the NRA? How does someone with the military training he's had become anti-gun?'

'There's no point in looking for logic in his actions,' said Yokely.

'He's crazy, right? He doesn't know what he's doing?'

'He's able to function, there's no question of that. He still has his skill set. What he's doing looks irrational to us, but he's probably convinced that he's doing the right thing.' Yokely sipped his whisky. 'But all that matters is that we stop him. I need to get the FBI's Emergency Planning Pack for the Kansas City Convention Centre. The FBI draws one up for every potential terrorist target.'

'I'll see what I can do,' said Lancaster.

'And you and I need to get to Kansas City. When is the NRA meeting?'

'Three days away.'

'Then as I'm always being told, the clock is ticking.'

It was almost midnight by the time Lancaster had downloaded the emergency planning pack to his laptop. It contained everything needed to defend or re-take a target attacked by terrorists, including satellite and ground-level photographs of the site and every installation on it, site-maps, building plans, construction specifications, wiring diagrams and the routes of conduits and storm-drains. It was a massive target to defend, eight city blocks square, with almost 400,000 square feet of unbroken exhibition space, 48 separate meeting rooms, and a main auditorium holding 4,000 people. The complex was connected to parking lots and the major downtown hotels by skywalks and underground walkways.

The two men studied it until the early hours, then grabbed a few hours sleep before catching an early morning flight to Kansas City.

CHAPTER 27

Yokely and Lancaster had only just checked into the Marriott Hotel in Kansas City when news came in that a gas-tanker packed with ammonium nitrate weedkiller and fuel oil had exploded on a back road three miles from Sedalia, Missouri. What little was left of the driver was burned beyond recognition, but crime scene investigators established that he had been a male African-American and turned up a partial fingerprint in the shattered cab of the truck. It was matched to Earl Long's prints.

It was high-fives time at the FBI, but Yokely flatly refused to believe that Long was dead. The chosen method: a truck packed with ANFO, had come close to success at the NRA convention the previous year, but with the authorities alerted by that incident, such a method was too crude to have had any chance of penetrating or destroying a well-defended target like the Kansas City Convention Centre.

Yokely was convinced that the truck was a distraction, and he phoned Senator Adams to say just that. 'I'm convinced that the body that was found was just that of a drifter or some other hapless victim snatched from the streets,' Yokely said.

The Senator said he was sure that Earl Long was dead but agreed that a strong military guard would be maintained at the Kansas City convention centre. The NRA normally took pride in allowing anyone complying with their state laws to enter their annual meeting carrying their arms, and attendees were still free to do so among the acres of weapons, accessories and everything else the most demanding gun nut could demand out in the exhibition areas. However, because the Vice President would be addressing the NRA's Leadership Forum, attendees would have to check in their weapons before entering the auditorium where it was to be held, creating the most heavily weaponised cloakroom in human history.

Security scanners were being set up between the concession area where the delegates could carry arms and the auditorium, and signs were being fixed to the walls of the walkways and escalators leading to it: 'Due to the attendance of the Vice President of the United States at this year's NRA-ILA Leadership Forum, the US Secret Service will be responsible for event security at the Arena. As a result, firearms and firearms accessories, knives or weapons of any kind will be prohibited in the Forum prior to and during his attendance. This Arena is under the jurisdiction of the US Secret Service during the Leadership Forum. By entering the area you are consenting to a search of your person and belongings.' There was a list of items that were prohibited in the auditorium, including backpacks, firearms, ammunition, drones, knives, laser pointers and selfie sticks.

'Here's what I don't understand,' said Lancaster. He smiled ruefully. 'Actually, there's a lot about this I don't understand. But the convention centre is so well protected, he's not going to be able to get a bomb in there. Or a gun.' He frowned. 'Is he planning to detonate a truckload of explosives again? Because that didn't work last time.'

'It's possible,' said Yokely. 'He could be planning to go out in a blaze of glory. Timothy McVeigh killed 168 people and injured almost seven hundred more with his truck bomb in Oklahoma City. But he came out of the blue. There's no way Long is going to be able to drive up to the convention centre with a truckload of explosives. He has to have something else planned.'

'Like what?'

Yokely flashed him a tight smile. 'That, my friend, is the sixty-four thousand dollar question.' He rubbed his chin as he looked at the FBI agent's laptop screen. 'How many men will there be in the VP's security detail?'

'At least twenty-four.'

'Can you get us in with them?'

Lancaster frowned. 'Do you think the VP is Long's target?'

'It's possible. I don't see that he can attack the whole venue, in which case he's after one target. And that target would probably be the VP.'

Lancaster nodded. 'I'll see what I can do.'

CHAPTER 28

Shorty arrived in Kansas City the day before the NRA annual meeting opened there. He took one of the few remaining rooms at one of the hotels linked by a walkway to the convention centre. As soon as he'd checked in, using a false identity and keeping his head lowered as he passed the CCTV cameras at the entrance, he began carrying out surveillance on the other people arriving for the convention. Most of the early arrivals were people working for arms companies or other manufacturers and retailers with stands in the trade area of the convention, where every conceivable kind of weapon, ammunition and shooting accessory was on display. Shorty briefly considered targeting one of them as his passport into the auditorium when the time came, but felt that their absence from their stands would be more likely to draw attention and instead he focussed on the NRA delegates who were beginning to check in for the convention itself. The NRA's membership was mostly white but there were enough black attendees for Shorty to be confident of finding one he could use as cover.

There were few delegates among the arrivals at first, but by the afternoon of that day, they were flooding in. Shorty soon identified a promising looking target, a black delegate who had booked into the same hotel. Although a few years older, he was of similar build and broadly similar looks. Shorty noted that the man was travelling alone and there was no obvious sign of friends or business associates waiting for him. Shorty waited in the hotel foyer, choosing a seat with a view of the elevators and the entrance to the bar, and in the early evening he caught sight of his potential target making his way to the bar. He watched him for a few minutes, making sure he was alone before he moved in. He took the bar-stool next to him, ordered a drink and then looked around and said 'Are we the only two black guys attending this thing?'

The other man laughed. 'It sure seems that way, don't it?'

'Mind if I join you?'

'Help yourself, I'm not expecting anyone. The name's James.'

'Jules.'

'Jules? As in 20,000 Leagues Under The Sea? Your old man must have loved Jules Verne, right?'

'I guess he did at that. Can I freshen that drink for you?'

'So what do you do for a living, James?' Shorty said, when they'd got their drinks.

'I'm in business up in Pittsburgh, just in a small way, but it gives me a good living. I have a gunshop.'

'Then you're in the right place, aren't you? And this'll all be tax deductible expenses too, will it?'

James grinned. 'You betcha it is.'

'And are you going to hear the Vice President speak?'

'I certainly am. My daddy'll be turning in his grave at the thought of me listening to a Republican - he was a lifelong Democrat - but to my mind the guy talks a lot of sense about this country.'

Shorty kept him chatting, plying him with drinks and waiting his chance. He planned to strike as soon as James went to the rest room or got in the elevator to go to his room.

All was going to plan, with James getting increasingly drunk, until a husky female voice interrupted their conversation. 'Hi there. You boys looking to party?'

James swivelled on his bar stool and looked her up and down. His expression showed that he was liking what he was seeing. She was not a natural blonde, her roots showing dark brown flecked with grey, but she was curvaceous and with her heavy make-up and the flattering low light of the bar, she could just about have passed for thirty.

'I don't know about my friend here,' James said, 'but I sure as hell am. Buy you a drink?'

'Sure,' she said, 'unless you'd rather we go and see what you've got in your minibar.'

James's smile broadened still further. 'Say Jules, would you mind if ...?'

Shorty masked his irritation and shook his head. 'Hell no, not at all. You go right ahead, I've got some calls to make anyhow. You two have fun now.'

He watched them heading for the elevators and then began casting around for a different target but although he sat there long enough to catch sight of the hooker coming out of the elevator again an hour later, he could not see any suitable alternative to James. There were very few African-American delegates at this hotel, and the only ones he saw were much older or younger than him, making any attempt to pass himself off as them too risky.

He waited another hour, in case James returned to the bar, but there was no sign of him and eventually Shorty wrote off the rest of the day and went up to his own room. It was a frustrating end to the day, but he told himself that he didn't need to be inside the auditorium on the opening day of the annual meeting anyway, just as long as he was in there in time to strike on the last day.

He spent most of the next day moving around the convention centre, looking for potential victims and keeping a discreet eye on the security at the barriers leading to the auditorium, checking the routine of the guards and looking for flaws and weak points in the security. He noticed that one of the guards manning the row of metal detectors and X-ray scanners at the security barrier spent most of his time chatting to the others at either side of him and barely glanced at the ID that delegates were showing him as they headed into the auditorium. Shorty made up his mind to use that guard's station to pass through the barrier the next day.

Just after lunchtime, he caught sight of James wandering around the trade fair and pausing to chat with the salesmen on a couple of the stands. Shorty tracked him, waiting until he was again strolling along one of the aisles, and then contrived to bump into him. 'Hi James,' he said. 'You hitting the bar again tonight? You never know, you might drop lucky again!'

'Luck had nothing to do with it, my friend,' James said with a smile. 'Just good looks and charm, but yeah, I'll be there.'

'Great, catch you later,' Shorty said and moved on.

By late afternoon, he was back in the hotel bar, sipping a glass of iced water as he waited for James to reappear. As soon as he did so, anxious to avoid being interrupted again by hookers looking for trade, Shorty walked over to his table, greeted him like a long lost friend and slapped him on the back. 'Hi there James, now give me the skinny on that broad I saw you disappearing with last night,' he said. 'I was still in the bar when she came down later on and from the smile on her face, I'd say she was a woman who had no complaints at all!'

He watched James's chest puff up as he soaked up the flattery. 'Now let me freshen that drink for you,' Shorty said, 'while I'm getting another for myself.' He made a brief show of trying to catch the eye of the waiter, then shrugged and said 'Too many thirsty people, I'll get the drinks myself.'

He walked up to the bar, gave his order and glanced behind him to check that James was still in his seat. When the barman brought the drinks, Shorty tipped him five bucks and waited until the barman moved on to the next customer, before taking a small glass phial from his breast pocket. Palming it to conceal it inside his hand and keeping a careful eye on the barman, he tipped the contents of the phial into James's glass. He swirled it around, clinking the ice cubes, then dropped the phial on the carpet and crushed it under his heel as he turned and headed back to the table.

When he sat down, he raised his glass. 'Well here's to new friends, good sales and bad women!'

He watched James take a gulp from his drink and then settled down to keep him occupied with small talk while he waited for the drug to take effect. Not long after downing the drink, James began to feel very drunk indeed, slurring his words and being very unsteady on his feet. 'Jeez,' he said. 'I don't know what the gin was in that last martini but it must have been rocket fuel; it's certainly doing a job on me. I think I need to take a break and freshen myself up.'

'I know what you mean,' Shorty said. 'I could sure do with a breather myself.'

He helped James to the elevator and supported him while he staggered along the corridor and fumbled for his room key. He dropped it on the floor and Shorty retrieved it, holding James upright with his other hand. By now James was so far gone that as he stumbled into his room, he might not even have been aware that Shorty had entered the room behind him. Shorty silently closed and locked the door and a moment later he broke James's neck with a savage jerk of his head.

He searched through James's pockets, found his wallet in his breast pocket and took his ID and his ticket for the auditorium where the keynote speeches and the Leadership Forum, addressed by the US Vice President, were to be held. Then he dumped the body in the bathroom, hung the 'Privacy Requested' sign on the door and, rather than returning to his own room, he lay down to sleep on the bed. If anyone came looking for James or any of the hotel staff tried to access the room, it would be better if he was there to deal with it. If he left the room and the body was then found, the unexplained murder might lead to heightened security around the convention centre and would certainly make using James's ID and ticket a much more risky exercise.

He remained in the room throughout the next day, ordering food from room service. The phone rang twice but he let it ring out without answering it, and when the chambermaid ignored the privacy sign and, receiving no reply, tried to unlock the door with her pass key so she could service the room, he shouted 'I asked for privacy goddammit. Can't you people read?' and she hurried away.

The next morning, the last day of the NRA Annual Meeting, Shorty was up early. When he left the room, the Privacy Requested sign was still hanging on the door. It would be mid- to late-afternoon by the time the chambermaid knocked again on the door and, getting no answer, would eventually enter the room and discover the body, and by then it would all be over, with Shorty either dead or long gone.

CHAPTER 29

O n the morning of the NRA's annual meeting, Yokely and Lancaster stationed themselves near the security scanners just outside the auditorium. They had Secret Service pins attached to their lapels and had earpieces and radios so that they could monitor the security detail's conversations. They had also been issued with VIP 'access all areas' badges that allowed them to roam the floor of the auditorium and also get into the 'Ring of Freedom' hospitality area where the NRA's great and good and their guests could refresh themselves.

The preliminary speeches were over and in the interval before the main event, a large number of delegates had come out of the auditorium to use the rest rooms or pick up a snack, a coffee or a beer before heading back in. Drinks were allowed in the auditorium but only in plastic glasses or paper cups, and mobs of people clutching disposable plates, cups and glasses, were milling around the security, jostling and anxious to get back in before the Vice President made his grand entrance. Most of the delegates were white, many carrying placards or banners and wearing baseball caps, shapeless plus-size blue jeans and sweat shirts emblazoned with NRA mottos or 'good ol' boy' slogans like 'The South Shall Rise Again.'

Unlike the rest of the day's attendees, the Vice President's armed Secret Service security detail weren't required to hand in their weapons before entering the auditorium. Yokely and Lancaster had also been given special dispensation to carry weapons. Yokely was carrying a Remington 9mm, a durable, very reliable semi-auto that packed serious firepower, holding eighteen rounds in its double-stack magazine and one in the chamber. Lancaster favoured the Glock and both had underarm holsters.

As always with US Secret Service bodyguard details, when they arrived, they simply barged everyone out of the way, scattering delegates, spilling drinks and food and setting off the security scanners right left and centre as they pushed their way through them, surrounding the Vice President. Yokely and Lancaster joined on to the back of the phalanx of security men, slipping through the scanners. The noise of the alarm as the scanner detected the weapon was lost in the deafening clamour from the other alarms. The guard manning the scanners just saw yet another of the phalanx of security men flanking the Vice President and switched his gaze back to the delegates who had been pushed aside and were now once more jostling each other as they tried to get through security.

Once inside the auditorium, Yokely and Lancaster took up a stance a little away from the Secret Service men, scanning the audience. Yokely's every sense was on maximum alert as his gaze raked the banked rows of seating in the auditorium, moving on row by row, and seat by seat, looking for the least thing that was unusual or out of place. Fewer than one in ten were African Americans and it took only a few minutes to reassure themselves that Earl Long wasn't there.

Yokely was confident that there was no explosive device hidden in the arena. At his insistence, reinforced by a command from the Senator, just that morning the arena had been swept by sniffer dogs for a second time. The local police chief's complaint that 'We already did that yesterday,' was brushed aside. 'That was yesterday. This is today, so do it again.' FBI technicians operating the latest high-tech sensors, so sensitive that, by sampling the air, they could detect the presence of every known explosive in concentrations as little as a few parts per million, had also swept the auditorium and pronounced it clear.

If there was a threat - and Yokely was still sure that there was - it would almost certainly come from a firearm. However it was unlikely that Long would be simply sitting with the general audience in the main body of the arena, just because the risk of being spotted, jostled or overpowered by other audience members as he tried to take his shot was too great. So Yokely concentrated most of his attention on the stairs, walkways, pillars and balconies.

The Vice President was now waiting in an ante-room, out of sight, while the NRA President prepared to give his warm up speech before introducing him.

Yokely looked up at the executive booths on the balcony where some of the NRA's heavy hitters and their celebrity friends were seated. While the routine business of the conference was being transacted, the booths had remained largely empty, but now, with the NRA President approaching the podium and the US Vice President about to appear, the NRA's favoured supporters and large donors were returning to their places. Yokely could see figures outlined momentarily against the low lighting in the booths as they settled themselves in their seats. Only one remained in darkness, apparently empty. The companies and individuals who had hired the booths had been checked out by the Secret Service and there had been no red flags. All twelve had been hired by corporate executives or wealthy individuals with well-established ties to the NRA.' He frowned as he ran his eyes along the line of booths. There were thirteen.

He nodded at Lancaster. 'Tell me I'm not going crazy. There are twelve booths, right?'

'Sure.' He looked up and counted them off, frowning when he got to thirteen. 'Shit. How did that happen?'

Yokely felt the familiar jolt of adrenaline - the body's natural fight or flight mechanism - but his heartbeat remained steady

'No, wait,' said Lancaster. 'There is a thirteenth but it isn't hired out. It was down on the plans as Security and Administration.' He gestured up at the box on the far left, which was in darkness. 'It's that one, the one that isn't being used.'

'I'm going up there,' said Yokely.

'Do you want me with you?'

'No, you stay down here, close to the VP,' said Yokely.

The NRA President was standing at the lectern and wrapping up his warm-up speech. As Yokely climbed the stairs, heading for the booth, he heard the President's voice rise an octave as he said 'Ladies and Gentlemen, it gives me the greatest pleasure to introduce a great friend of mine and a true supporter of the NRA, the Vice President of the United States!'

The audience rose to give him a standing ovation as he strode across the platform, shaking hands with the NRA President and smiling and waving to the crowd. Yokely was confident that while the audience was on their feet and the Vice President was moving across the stage, the assassin would not have a clear shot. When the applause subsided and the Vice President stood motionless at the lectern had to be the moment when Earl Long would take his shot.

CHAPTER 30

Shorty had been one of the first through the security scanners when the auditorium opened for
the day several hours earlier. He was unarmed and
strolled into the auditorium unchallenged after
showing his stolen ID and ticket. Once there, he had
made his way up the stairs and slipped into the booth
when no one was within sight. He waited, impassive,
in the darkness, watching as the crowds slowly fil-
tered into the auditorium and the rows began to fill,
only stirring himself when the first speeches began
and the audience noise rose.

Between the balcony rail and the floor, the front
of the booth was covered in plywood, decorated with
wood mouldings and stained to give it a look like oak
panelling, at least in the dim light of the booth. Shorty
waited until the audience noise swelled into a roar of
acclamation as one of the NRA's celebrity supporters
- a cowboy actor from the heyday of Hollywood 'horse
opera' movies - took to the stage. The cheers and
applause drowned the noise as Shorty swung his boot
and smashed through the fake panelling. He waited

for the next ovation to cover the noise as he tore away the splintered wood, exposing what lay hidden behind it: a Sig-Sauer sniper's rifle with a telescopic sight. Next to it was a box of ammunition, though he wasn't anticipating having time - or need - to fire more than two or three shots. He had hidden the weapon some twelve months earlier when he had been working as a contractor on the site. The NRA planned its annual meetings two years in advance so he had known that the venue was going to be used and had managed to get himself on a construction team working on renovations to the convention centre.

Whether he could escape in the subsequent panic and confusion, or would be arrested or killed, no longer mattered to him. This was the endgame he had been working towards. If he could not eliminate the entire NRA leadership, he could at least remove its figurehead and its tame creature in the White House. He eased the rifle out of its hiding place, loaded the clip and worked the action to load a round into the chamber. Normally he would have used a low tripod to brace the barrel, but the padded balcony rail would serve just as well.

Such were his sniping skills on the open air ranges that, allowing for the wind speed and the pull of gravity on the round, he could knock the eye out of a target at a range of up to three quarters of a mile. With that pedigree, a shot of no more than 150 yards in the still air of an enclosed space like the auditorium would be almost childishly simple.

As the Vice President reached the podium and stood acknowledging the applause, Shorty eased the rifle forward, resting the barrel on the balcony rail. He pressed his eye to the sniper scope and found his target. The Vice President's head was still in plain view, showing above the autocue and the bullet-proof lectern shielding the rest of him. Shorty began increasing the magnification until the bridge of the Vice President's nose and part of his right eye completely filled his vision.

Chapter 31

Yokely saw a slim black shape slide out over the balcony rail of the darkened booth. He ran up the rest of the stairs and along the corridor behind the booths, bowling over a latecomer, hurrying to take his place for the Vice President's speech. Yokely drew his pistol as he ran, paused for an instant outside the door of the box, then threw himself at the door of the booth.

As Yokely hurled himself against the door, it gave a little but then rebounded. Shorty had piled up the table and chairs in the booth against the door, creating a makeshift barricade. The edge of the door struck Yokely's wrist, trapping it against the frame. He felt a stab of agonising pain and the pistol slipped from his grasp, dropping to the floor on the inside of the door. He pushed the door again and it gave. Then he stepped back and kicked it, hard. The door opened just enough for Yokely to be able to squeeze through.

Shorty had been hunched over the rifle, with the Vice President's eye and nose filling his sights and he was just taking up the first pressure on the trigger when he heard the crash of splintering wood behind him. He ignored the interruption and concentrated on his target. He zeroed in on the VP's face, exhaled and began to squeeze the trigger.

Yokely forced his way into the room. A chair tipped over and he kicked it towards the shooter. The chair hit Shorty just as he pulled the trigger and the round flew high and wide, punching a hole through the Stars and Stripes draped across the backdrop of the stage behind the Vice President.

Shorty twisted around, his face contorted into a snarl. He brought his rifle up but Yokely threw himself to the side and the round flashed over his head, blowing a hole in the partition that divided the booth from the next one. Before Shorty could fire again, Yokely was on him, launching himself into a dive that sent his shoulder smashing into Shorty's ribs.

The auditorium below them was dissolving into panic and chaos. While the NRA President ducked behind the podium, and sat hunched there, shaking with fright, the Secret Service bodyguards rushed to shield the Vice President and then began to hustle him off the stage. The panicked audience members scrambled over, trampled and fought with each other as they stampeded for the exits.

Because of the Secret Service restrictions, none of the NRA members were armed but as the first ones scrambled out of the arena, with most just fleeing in panic, others besieged the cloakrooms, screaming for their weapons. A handful grabbed their hand-guns and headed back into the auditorium, where the NRA President was still cowering behind the bullet-proof lectern. Two NRA members entering from opposite sides of the auditorium clutching their weapons, mistook each other for the assassin and fired simultaneously. Neither was hit, but the fresh gunfire only added to the panic.

Shorty swung the butt of his rifle at Yokely's head, but it was an unwieldy weapon and he dodged the blow, and followed up with a short-arm punch aimed at crushing Shorty's Adam's apple. Shorty dropped his chin to minimise the impact and then swung his own elbow, catching Yokely high on the temple.

Yokely shook his head to clear it, dodged another punch and launched himself again, hitting Shorty low, at the midpoint of the thighs. The impact sent him sprawling across Yokely's back and they crashed onto the edge of the balcony together. Yokely smashed his elbow back at Shorty's head and twisted around, grasping at the gun arm, as Shorty's other hand clawed at Yokely's eyes.

'Give it up,' Yokely said, choking on the words as Shorty wrenched his left arm free and chopped at his throat. The other man's weight still lay across him, but Yokely brought up his knee, jackknifing it into Shorty's groin. As the breath whistled from his lungs, Yokely swung him over to the side and smashed Shorty's arm down onto the balcony rail. The rifle fired again, and a round ripped through the ceiling of the auditorium, but Shorty let go of the weapon and it slid over the rail and disappeared into the auditorium.

Shorty's fingers closed around Yokely's throat and he twisted from side to side, punching at Shorty's head, but he couldn't break the grip. The blood pounded in his veins and he heard a roaring in his ears as Shorty's face, inches from his own, began to blur.

Dredging up his last reserves, Yokely smashed his forehead into the bridge of Shorty's nose. His mouth opened in a grunt of pain and Yokely felt the fingers at his throat relax their grip for a second. He twisted and moved sideways, breaking the hold on his neck, but even as he grabbed Shorty's wrist and tried to force it away, he found himself once more pinned against the other man's body. The balcony rail was pressing against his back but Shorty was still pushing against him and still locked together, they slid over the edge and plunged towards the floor of the auditorium.

Time seemed to slow. Yokely heard screams that sounded like they came from the bottom of a well. He stared at Shorty with a curious detachment but then time accelerated again in a frightening blur of speed and noise. Yokely grunted and heaved at Shorty with all the strength he possessed, twisting him around in midair.

There was a thud that echoed from the walls and the crack of breaking bone as Shorty's body smashed down onto the floor of the auditorium. Even with Shorty's body to absorb some of the impact, Yokely felt the breath explode from his own lungs as he was crushed down into Shorty's body, and he blacked out for a few seconds. When he opened his eyes, he saw Lancaster standing over him. 'It's all right,' Yokely gasped, still struggling for breath. 'I'm okay. He took the worst of the impact.'

Shorty's eyes flickered open at the sound of Yokely's voice. His eyes showed that he knew it was the end. 'I can't move my legs,' he said.

Yokely sat up. Shorty coughed and swallowed as blood filled his mouth. His hand grasped Yokely's wrist. 'It's over,' he said. 'I'm done.'

Yokely nodded. 'Yeah.'

'They killed my daughter.' He coughed and more blood spilled out of his mouth.

'At least you'll be with her now,' said Yokely.

Shorty began to smile but then he shuddered and his eyes went blank. He was dead before the Secret Service agents reached them.

CHAPTER 32

Yokely broke three ribs in the fall and was badly bruised, but after an X-Ray at North Kansas City Hospital he was pronounced as well as could be expected after falling thirty feet onto a concrete floor, albeit cushioned by another body. Later that evening he was in Senator Adams's townhouse, drinking whiskey from a crystal tumbler and accepting the man's grateful thanks. 'The Vice President would like to meet you at some point, to thank you personally,' said the Senator.

'I don't need his thanks,' said Yokely. 'To be honest, I'm not a fan.'

The Senator smiled and raised his glass. 'Me neither.'

'The media is treating Earl Long as a mentally ill lone wolf,' said Yokely.

'Which is accurate,' said the Senator.

'But he hasn't been linked to the school shootings. Or the fire bombing. Just the killing of General Jackson.'

'The public will probably accept that Long was disturbed enough to assassinate General Jackson and attempt to kill the Vice President. But if we let it be known he was also behind the school shootings, then the racial element will kick in and as I said before we don't want to have to deal with the inevitable backlash.'

'But his DNA was found at one of the shooting scenes. That's how we identified him.'

'That information is not being made public,' said the Senator.

'So the school shootings will remain unsolved?'

'So far as the public is concerned, yes.'

'That will leave a lot of unhappy parents,' said Yokely.

'Do you think they would be any happier if they knew that their children were murdered by a mentally deranged former special forces soldier who was lashing out at the NRA and their supporters?'

Yokely shrugged. It wasn't a question he could answer.

'It's better handled this way,' said the Senator. He raised his glass in salute. 'Nice job, Richard.'

About The Author

Stephen Leather is one of the UK's most success-ful thriller writers, an eBook and *Sunday Times* bestseller and author of the critically acclaimed Dan "Spider" Shepherd series and the Jack Nightingale supernatural detective novels. Before becoming a novelist he was a journalist for more than ten years on newspapers such as *The Times*, the *Daily Mirror*, the *Glasgow Herald*, the *Daily Mail* and the *South China Morning Post* in Hong Kong. He is one of the coun-try's most successful eBook authors and his eBooks have topped the Amazon Kindle charts in the UK and the US. *The Bookseller* magazine named him as one of the 100 most influential people in the UK publishing world.

Born in Manchester, he began writing full-time in 1992. His bestsellers have been translated into fifteen languages. He has also written for television shows such as *London's Burning*, *The Knock* and the BBC's *Murder in Mind* series, Two of his novels, *The Stretch* and *The Bombmaker*, were filmed for TV and

The Chinaman is now a major motion picture starring Pierce Brosnan and Jackie Chan.

To find out more, you can visit his website at www.stephenleather.com.

THE RUNNER

*The explosive new stand-alone thriller from
the author of the Spider Shepherd series.*

Sally Page is an MI5 'footie', a junior Secret Service
Agent who maintains 'legends': fake identities
or footprints used by real spies. Her day consists of
maintaining flats and houses were the legends alleg-
edly live, doing online shopping, using payment,
loyalty and travel cards and going on social media in
their names - anything to give the impression to hostile surveillance that the legends are living, breathing
individuals.

One day she goes out for a coffee run from the safe
house from which she and her fellow footies operate.
When she comes back they have all been murdered
and she barely escapes with her own life. She is on
the run: but from whom she has no idea. Worse, her
bosses at MI5 seem powerless to help her. To live, she
will have to use all the lies and false identities she has
so carefully created while discovering the truth ...

Hodder and Stoughton have published sixteen books featuring Dan 'Spider' Shepherd written by *Sunday Times* bestselling author Stephen Leather. His standalone thriller *The Runner*, will be published in January 2020.

Printed in Great Britain
by Amazon